Bound Together

Eliza Jane

DEDICATION

To readers everywhere.

Chapter One

Zoey

I sat up in bed, groggy and tired. My mind registered that I only had a few days left until my class trip to Paris and that missing ounce of enthusiasm I needed propelled me out of bed. I threw on the closest pair of jeans and grey T-shirt that lay crumpled on my floor and swept my hair up into a messy bun on top of my head.

I opened doors as I moved down the hall, avoiding my parent's room. "Ty, Charlie, Pete, Cora –time for school." I jogged down the stairs, stepping over stray articles of clothes and discarded toys almost by instinct. An abandoned teddy bear winked up at me with one glass eye.

I did my best to clear the table of last night's homework and divided it into the backpacks hung by the back door, keeping out Pete's list of spelling words. I set a stack of bowls and the cereal and milk on the table and went to call up the stairs once more. My three younger brothers and little sister emerged one by one, messy-haired and tired and slid into their chairs around the table.

"Pete." He looked up in between bites of generic brand Cap'n Crunch. I consulted the spelling list. "Spell invention."

He swallowed the cereal roughly, and wiped away the milk rolling down his chin. "I—v"

"Take your time. Sound it out, innnvention," I hinted. He started again and I moved onto packing lunches while Pete spelled it correctly. "Ty, straight home after soccer practice tonight. I could use some help, I still have to pack." My fourteen-year-old brother and second in command looked up and nodded.

"There's a birthday party at the arcade after school today, Zoey," Charlie said. "I need five dollars for pizza."

"Fine." I went to our dad's Carhartt jacket hung by the door and dug through his pockets for the all the loose change I could find. "Here." I set the mountain of coins in front of Charlie. "Be home by six. I don't like you walking after dark."

I finished the bologna sandwiches and re-filled bottles of water for everyone then braided Cora's hair. We lived close enough to the school that we walked. Our town was so small that the elementary, middle and high schools were all in a row on the same street. I dropped off Pete and Cora at the elementary school, then Charlie and Ty at the middle school.

I headed into the high school, heard a shriek and spun around. Morgan grabbed my upper arms and began jumping up and down.

"What?" I looked at her.

"Brandon's parents out of town tonight! He's having a party at his place."

"So?"

"So, it's going to be epic and he personally invited me." She put her hand to her chest. "I think he digs my new blue streak." Morgan ran her fingers through the single blue highlight framing her face in otherwise lackluster blonde hair.

She pulled me into her dancing embrace.

"You know I'm not a good hugger." I squirmed out of her grasp.

Morgan rolled her eyes.

"I'm a pretty good side-hugger though, so hopefully that makes up for it," I said, squeezing her awkwardly with one arm.

She shrugged out of my half-embrace. "It's fine, Zoey. You'll come with me, right?"

"Tonight?"

"Yes, tonight—it's Friday night. Don't tell me you can't either. Your brothers and sister will be fine without you for one night."

"You'd think so, but when I go home to microwaved Barbie

dolls and a pregnant flea ridden cat, like last Friday—then I'd argue different."

She started walking and pulled me along towards our locker. "You're coming—don't try to get out of this. I'm sure Jordan's going," she said, like that would entice me. "What's up with you two anyway?"

I twisted the lock, entering our combination and popped the locker open. "Nothing really."

"Earth to Zoey." She waved her hand in front of my face, breaking my concentration from inspecting my textbooks. "You guys had sex," she whispered so loudly a few heads turned our way.

"Thanks for letting half of South Lake High in on that." I glanced over my shoulder, seeing who might have overheard, then decided I didn't care.

She ducked her head behind the door of our locker, pretending it was providing us the privacy we needed to have this conversation. "He's not your boyfriend?"

"Ah, Jordan? Last I checked, no." I laughed and slammed the locker shut. "He's, I don't know—a shiny object to distract me from my crappy life."

"God, Zoey, you're more emotionally crippled than I realize sometimes."

"Whatever, Morgan. Jordan's not exactly a prized catch if

you haven't noticed."

Just then Jordan walked up, his jeans sagging down low, dirty T-shirt hanging on his lanky frame, and a skateboard stuck through his backpack behind him. "Hey, Mamacita!" he said squeezing me to his side.

I wiggled my way free. "Hey," I returned.

"She's not good at hugging," Morgan leaned in to remind him.

"That's fine. I can think of a few things I like better than hugs." He winked at me.

"I gotta get to class." I turned and walked towards my AP Global Studies class, leaving them looking after me. I deliberately avoided making eye contact with any of my classmates as I passed through the hall, which I had down to such a science that they didn't bother with me either.

I sat down in my usual back row seat and took out my notebook. Mr. Rhinehart came in just as the bell rang and closed the door behind him, shutting Matt Parker, king of the jock-squad out in the hall. I didn't even understand why he was in this class; it certainly wasn't on the normal menu of classes for football players. This was the one class where I didn't feel like I stood out. I could raise my hand and answer questions and people didn't think I was a freak. Matt frowned and knocked on the door. I didn't think I'd ever seen him late before.

Mr. Rhinehart turned and unlocked the door. "Thank you for gracing us with your presence today, Mr. Parker. Take a seat."

Matt's normal section of front row seating was occupied, so he made his way to the back of the room and sat down next to me. He glanced at me once before dropping his eyes to the desk in front of him. He was wearing his jersey today, like all the football players did on game day. A vein stood out in his neck and I wondered if something had happened, maybe he'd been in a fight or something. Maybe Chelsey Martin had cheated on him again. Whatever—I didn't care. I turned my attention back to Mr. Rhinehart.

We were going to Paris in two days, and I couldn't wait to get out of this town and see something, even if it was only for eight days. It would be good practice for my family to learn to survive without me for when I went away to college next year. As much as I tried to remind everyone that I wasn't going to be around forever, I don't think they really realized what that was going to mean.

"Instead of having a regular lesson today," Mr. Rhinehart said. "We're going to talk about your assignment while we're abroad." He sat down on the edge of his desk, and his too tight khaki pants budged in all the wrong places. *Eww.* "As you know, this is a college-level placement course. We've spent the last few months learning culture, politics, art, and the social and economic conditions that have shaped the world we live in today. Your assignment while we're there other than having fun," he smiled at the class, "is to bring history alive. You will find a topic you wish to explore and write a ten-page paper, due two weeks after we return. You will do this in pairs of two."

He moved around the room, pointing at people sitting next to each other as he went. "Bobby and Brian. Amanda and Stephanie." He continued down the aisle, coming closer to the back of the room. I looked around me, and the only person near me was Matt. I wondered if I could quickly change seats. He couldn't possibly mean for me and Matt to work together. My mind went fuzzy as Mr. Rhinehart moved in slow motion towards us. No, this could not happen. This was not how I planned to spend my Euro-adventure, babysitting some over-pampered jock. "Zoey and Matt," he said passing between us. I knew my face contorted at the sounds of our names spoken together, but I didn't even care that he or Matt could see my look of disgust.

Matt looked at me, and then Mr. Rhinehart's back. "Ah, Mr. Rhinehart?" He stopped walking and turned to face us. "It's just I don't know if...Zoey and I should be partners on this assignment." He said my name like he didn't know it and was only reciting what Mr. Rhinehart had said a moment before. We'd gone to school together since first grade, what a douche. "Maybe I could be with Brian and she could be with Stephanie," he suggested.

"You're both grown-ups. Start acting like it." And with that he turned and headed for the front of the classroom. "You have thirty-seven minutes to plan out your assignment," he said glancing at the clock.

You. Have. Got. To. Be. Kidding. Me. I could tell Matt wasn't

7

happy about being paired together either, and that only made it worse. I avoided meeting his eyes, though I could tell he was looking at me. I fished around inside my backpack for a pen. My hand found something odd-shaped at the bottom and I pulled it out. It was Pete's inhaler. *How the hell did that get in here?* I hoped Pete would be okay without for the morning. I could bring it over to him at lunch.

"Zoey?" he said softly, breaking my concentration from the inhaler. "Are you…okay?"

I dropped the inhaler into my bag and took a deep breath. "Whatever. Let's get this over with."

Chapter Two

Matt

Zoey Marshall was looking at me like I was diseased. And was that a thing of pepper spray she was holding? She threw it back in her bag.

"So, um, did you have any ideas for the assignment?" I asked. She continued glaring at me for what felt like too long. I pulled my eyes away from hers and flipped open my European history book. "Should we just brainstorm some ideas together?" I offered. She didn't say anything, and began picking at her thumb nail. Flecks of purple polish fell onto the tile floor under her desk. What the hell was her problem? We were going to Europe, not detention. Why was she always so damn sulky? "Listen, I get that you're not happy about working with me. I know we're not exactly friends. But it's not like we have a choice now, do we?" She looked up at me like she wanted to say something, then closed her mouth.

I flipped open my notebook to a blank sheet of paper. "I had a few ideas, so I guess I'll start. Greek influence on French

Impressionism. Napoléon Bonaparte. King Louis." I wrote each idea down and looked up at her for a response. She looked down at the page, blinking at the words I'd written. I flipped through the pages in my textbook. "Imported goods and currency?" I offered. She didn't say anything, so I wrote it down on the paper. She was back to inspecting her thumb nail. The purple nail polish was nearly chipped off. I watched her peel the paint off her nail and drop it to the floor in little specks. She seemed a million miles away, zoned out on something. Dark circles shaded her eyes, but other than that her skin was perfectly clear and porcelain white. "Were you going to mace me before?"

"Huh?" She looked up at me suddenly.

"That bottle of spray you took out of your bag." I nodded to the backpack at her feet.

She twisted in her seat and kicked the bag further under her desk. "No," she scoffed. "That's my brother's inhaler. I don't know what it's doing in there."

"So did you have any ideas for our paper?" I held up the sheet bringing her attention back to the assignment. Getting into a conversation with her probably wasn't a wise idea.

"Whatever you want to do is fine with me. We can always just figure it out when we get there." She took out a sketch pad and charcoal pencil from her backpack and began sketching dark lines across the page. I watched the lines become a twisting, knotted branch as she worked.

"Remember, mandatory pre-trip meeting tomorrow at eleven a.m —my classroom. Bring a parent," Mr. Rhinehart called as the bell rang.

I had Advanced Weight Training next as my gym credit. Our whole varsity football team was in the class. It was basically a goof-off hour with weights. I went into the locker room and pulled off my jersey. I glanced in the mirror. My biceps were getting huge. I flexed in the mirror and was caught by Justin as he rounded the corner.

"Nice guns, man."

"Thanks," I pulled a shirt from my locker, sniffed it, then threw it on over my head. This morning had started off shitty. I'd had a run in with Chelsey in the hall just before first period. I'd broken up with her last night, but today she informed me that she'd cheated on me last weekend with Dave Cook, the safety on my team. It didn't matter—I was the one who ended things with her, so I shouldn't care.

"Hey bro, sorry about Chelsey. I heard what happened," Justin said without glancing over since we were both changing. He must have heard her version of why we broke up—the one that made it look like she did the breaking up.

"It's not a big deal," I said.

"She was hot, but she was kind of annoying," Justin said. "She had nice tits, though."

I gave him a *just drop it* look.

"What?" He held his hands up in surrender. "She did." He wasn't lying, the girl was stacked, but that was beside the point. I didn't know why I was with her and when I could no longer remember, I figured it was time to end it.

We hit the weight room and cranked up the stereo, Animal I Have Become by Three Days Grace blared from the speakers mounted in the corners. Justin and I went to the bench press and loaded it up with forty-fives while the rest of the guys stationed themselves around the room in groups of twos and threes.

"So you leave for your trip on Sunday, right?" he asked, getting into position first.

I stood behind him. "Yeah."

He took a deep breath and pulled the bar free, lowering it to his chest. He blew out a breath, pushing the bar up. He only made it eight reps before I had to help him re-rack the weight. He sat up and got off the bench. We switched positions.

Coach Dickey walked by, his white ball cap with the blue panther pulled down low over his forehead. "Don't work too hard today, I want you guys fresh for tonight's game." He patted my shoulder.

I leaned back on the bench and pushed the bar straight up, locking my elbows before lowering the weight down towards me. I did fifteen reps, puffing my breath out as I lowered the bar each time, then re-racked it myself.

"Damn. You're an animal, man." Justin slapped my back when I sat up. We did a few more sets, then stretched on the mats before hitting the showers early. Coach pretty much expected us to slack off on game days. "You know, I think it's better that you and Chelsey aren't together anymore," Justin said from across the locker room. I glanced over at him. "Paris a romantic country you know," he said.

"It's a city—not a country," I corrected.

"Whatever. I just mean now you won't be tied down — you're free to hook up who whoever you want on this trip."

I wasn't planning to hook up with anyone, I just figured it would be my one chance to get out of this town and see the world, before I stuck around after high school to take over my parent's tire store. "I got paired up with Zoey Marshall on our assignment while we're there."

"Zoey who?" Justin asked.

"That goth girl, always wears black, doesn't talk much. She sits with Morgan at lunch. I think she might be dating Jordan Redding." I wondered how I knew so much about a girl I supposedly never noticed.

"Is she hot?" Justin asked.

I thought about it for a second. I'd never seen her looking put together, but she did look better without loads of make-up, like Chelsey always wore. She had long dark hair and bright sky blue eyes, but I knew the right answer, the answer according to Justin would be no. "Naw, not really," I shook my head.

"Well, who cares, you know? What happens on class trips stays on class trips," he laughed.

Only I knew nothing would be happening between me and Zoey in Paris. We'd be lucky if we could survive the week and get our assignment done. She gave off very clear signals—and that signal was eff off.

Chapter Three

Zoey

During lunch I jogged over to the elementary school and dropped Pete's inhaler off with the nurse. I didn't have enough time to eat, so I grabbed a bag of pretzels on my way back and headed to fourth period, Calculus. I listened to Ms. Ashby drone on about functions and tangent lines while I tried to chew my pretzels as quietly as possible and thought about my assignment with Matt. I'd figured he would've tried to make me do all the work on our assignment, but he surprised me when he took out his books and started jotting down his own ideas. His writing was really neat too, with small, perfectly shaped letters.

Ms. Ashby heard me reach my hand into the bag, and her head has turned from the white board to the back of the room where I was sitting. "Zoey—no food in class. You know that."

I swallowed down the pretzel. "Yeah, sorry, I didn't get to eat during lunch."

"It's your responsibility to plan your time better so you can eat during your lunch period. Put it away," she said with no sympathy in her voice.

I knew it was no use explaining why I couldn't eat during lunch, so I shoved one last pretzel in my mouth then folded the bag up and stuck it in my backpack.

*****

After school I had an hour before the kids got out of school. This was usually the time I went to my mom's room to get her up. My dad worked two to midnight at the sheet metal factory, so it pretty much meant we didn't see him during the week. And depending on the kind of day my mom was having determined if she'd be up and around, wandering around the house without a purpose, or if she'd be a zombie, barely getting out of bed to eat or shower. After these last few years of watching her pull away from us, I would have preferred to just leave her alone in her room, but the kids got worried if she wasn't out of bed by the time they got home.

I dropped my bag by the door and kicked off my Converse. It was eerily silent in the house, and I dreaded going into her room. I didn't like the feeling of coming home and not knowing what I'd find. At this point though, I'd pretty much given up hope for her getting better and was no longer going to be the one to try and single-handedly pull her out of this. She needed to want to get help and my dad needed to care enough to get involved too; I'd been through this too many times before and did my best now to act like I didn't care at all.

I could hear her TV was on through the closed door. I put my hand on the knob. "Mom?" I opened the door slowly. She was sitting up in bed. The air in the room smelled stale and it was dim with the dusty curtains pulled shut.

"Hi, baby," she said. Her hair was stringy and tried to remember if she'd showered yesterday.

I went to the window and pulled apart the curtains, securing them in the tie-backs. "The kids are going to be home soon. Come on and get up. I'll make you some coffee."

"What would I do without you?" she asked as I was leaving the room.

"Um, raise your own kids?" I uttered under my breath so low she couldn't hear me. I hated being in there.

I went to the kitchen and went through my routine without thinking. I rinsed the day-old coffee from the pot and started a fresh pot, then got the kids' after school snack ready, celery and peanut butter today, even though they'd complain. And soon the house was filled the sounds of the kids again and I relaxed a little. I busied myself sorting Ty's soccer gear and piles of laundry for the Laundromat tomorrow, I helped Cora search for her missing hamster until she realized that she'd left him in his plastic ball all night and we put him back in his cage.

And then it was time to start dinner. It was Friday, which I'd dubbed Spaghetti Spectacular night. It was easier to have set days for dinner, cutting down on time spent meal planning. I dumped the box of pasta into boiling water and buttered six slices of white bread. When it was ready, we ate without Charlie, though I wasn't surprised he'd ignored my six o'clock curfew —he'd reminded me many times these past few months that I wasn't his mom. Around seven when he still wasn't home, I sent Ty out to look for him at the arcade. They showed up a little while later, after sneaking in a few more games I'm sure.

I collapsed on the couch to watch a Disney princess movie with Cora before it was time for bed. She took a bath around eight, then cuddled with Mom in her room before I went in to reinforce lights out at nine. Why was it that I got all the shit work while Mom picked and chose when she wanted to parent?

I went to my room and fell back onto the bed. I normally kept my room pretty neat, but piles of clothes and books were invading what little floor space I had. I folded the flattened pillow in half rather than trying to fluff it up and closed my eyes. My cell phone buzzed on my night stand and I picked it up. It was Morgan.

"Hello?"

"Hey Zoey —we're just leaving the game for Brandon's. Are you ready or what?"

"Uhh," I tried to stall for more time.

"We'll swing by and get you. Right, Brian?" I heard him groan on the other end.

I'd completely spaced on the party tonight. I tried to remember if I'd actually agreed to go. I knew I could probably go if I wanted to…I don't know—it just didn't sound fun. I had nothing in common with the kids that would be there. They wouldn't understand my life, so I figured it was better not to get involved. That way I'd never have to explain away my family, I'd never have to be ashamed over this. This didn't define me. It wasn't who I was. I'd never even let Morgan come inside before. I didn't want her to see my messy house, me in 'Mom-mode', and risk her seeing what my Mom was really like. It was better this way. I'd be gone from all this next year.

I heard yelling coming from down the hall. "Hang on, Morgan." I headed for Charlie and Pete's room where they were most likely in another fight about whose turn it was on the Nintendo DS. I found Pete curled up in the fetal position on the lower bunk, struggling to breathe. "Gotta go!" I called before hanging up on Morgan.

"Where's his inhaler?" I yelled to Charlie.

"He said he left it at school," Charlie said, his voice high, his eyes pleading with me to do something, to fix it.

"Okay–it's okay," I said to reassure them as much as myself.

Pete's breathing was loud, labored and I pulled him up to sitting. I tried to calm him, smoothing my hand up and down his back but he was really struggling. I held my hands in an imaginary cup under his nose, remembering the game I'd made up last year when we ran out of his inhaler medication. "Smell the hot chocolate," I told him. He breathed in through his nose. "And blow on it cause it's hot." He blew a little puff of air at my hands. "Good. Smell the hot chocolate." He breathed in again, less strained this time.

My phone was buzzing again at my feet. I kicked it over to Charlie. "Answer it for me and hold it up to my ear." Charlie did as he was told. I kept my hands formed into a cup in front of Pete. "Hey Morgan—sorry, Pete had an asthma attack. I'm not going to be able to go out tonight."

She was disappointed, but didn't sound mad. I'm sure the promise of hanging out with Brandon was part of the reason.

After reading them a few stories, and making sure Pete's breathing was completely back to normal, I went back to my room and dug around in the closet for a suitcase. I didn't get very far on packing though, figuring I would need to wait until after I finished the laundry tomorrow.

My cell was buzzing again and I crawled over on my hands and knees to answer it. It was a text from Jordan.

Im outside. Let me in.

I went to my window and sure enough, Jordan's car was

parked on the street in front of my house. What was he doing here? I looked at the clock —it was after eleven.

Is this a booty call? I texted back.

Haha. Maybe. He wrote. *Come down.* His next note said.

Since there was no way I was letting him come inside, I texted him back. *K.* I hit send and jogged down the stairs and out the front door.

He pushed open the passenger side door for me as I walked up the car. I climbed in and he wasted no time leaning over to give me a kiss. I could tell he'd been drinking.

"Geez, Jordan—slobber much?" I pushed him back to his seat. He grinned at me stupidly. "How was Brandon's party?" I asked.

"It was cool. I missed you though." He put his hand on my knee.

"You wanted a piece is more like it." I resisted the urge to move his hand away.

"So what's the deal with us, huh Zoey?" His brow crinkled in concentration as he studied me. The look on his face told me he was seeing me with double vision. He blinked and shook his head.

"What do you mean?" I asked, like I had no idea what he was talking about.

"Why'd we have sex last weekend?" he whispered, even

though we were alone in his car with no chance of anyone overhearing us. The truth was I had no idea why we had sex. I guess it was just me pretending to be a normal seventeen-year-old last Friday night, and if that meant drinking a little and making out with a guy from my class, that's exactly what I wanted to do.

I hadn't expected us to go all the way, but it had been like a strange game of chicken, and neither of us wanted to be the one to stop it. It had been everything I'd assumed my first time would be: clumsy, awkward, and a little painful. Which was probably best anyway, since I never had illusions of being in love my first time. I figured it was best to get the awkward first time out of the way with someone that didn't matter.

He trailed his hand over my thigh. "It was my first time, I didn't tell you before —but I wanted you to know," he said.

"That's nice," I said. I had no intention of telling him he was my first too. I didn't want him to think it meant something it didn't.

He picked up my hand and interlaced his fingers with mine. "I can't stop thinking about you," he breathed onto my neck.

"Can't stop thinking about me or about the sex?" I questioned.

"Well, that *was* fun." He moved up to my ear.

"Why'd you come here?

"I like you, Zoey," he continued kissing my neck.

"You don't even know me, Jordan." I pushed him back for a second. "Besides, I don't have time for a boyfriend right now." He looked at me for a second before falling in towards me again. "Jordan, did you hear me?"

"Yeah. That's cool—I just thought we could still, ya know?" He trailed his fingers up my thigh.

The clock on his dash said 11:27. "My dad will be home from work soon."

He glanced at the clock and smirked. "I promise it'll be quick."

"Hmm. As tempting as that sounds—I'm gonna pass. Thanks though." I pulled the handle, opening the door and the cool night air seemed to have some effect at bringing him back to his senses.

"Have fun on your trip, Zoey!" he called as I swung the door shut.

I climbed the stairs to my room, and since I was still up, I figured I might as well wait up for my dad to get home. But then I remembered it was Friday and he always went out for a drink with the guys after work on Fridays. I wasn't tired yet, so I sat down at my laptop. I logged into Facebook and scrolled through the pictures of people having fun, the updated posts about weekend plans.

I typed Matt Parker's name into the search bar and hit enter. I didn't even know why I was searching for him. His picture came up. He was in his white football uniform, holding a ball at his waist, a big smile on his face with his blonde hair and deep blue eyes. He had the small town, All American hero look down to a tee, his perfect boy features that were hard not to notice, especially in a high school filled with acne-ridden, greasy-haired boys. *I'm glad your life's so fucking perfect*, I thought. I closed my laptop.

Chapter Four

Matt

Okay, so I screwed up. During our pre-game warm-up, I'd tackled Dave Cook. Dave was third string; barely good enough to be on the team, and today the third string guys were mimicking the offense of the team we'd be playing tonight. We were running a practice play and I saw my opportunity, and I took it. I ran full speed towards him and slammed his ass into the ground right in front of where the cheerleaders were warming up. Chelsey's mouth had fallen open in a perfect O.

That earned me a lecture from Coach—Dave was a teammate, I was the captain, I had to set a good example, whatever. Instead telling Coach that Dave had slept with my girlfriend, I apologized said I didn't mean to hit him that hard. But damn it felt good.

"Roid rage?" Justin had asked when I'd jogged back to the huddle.

Now at Brandon Sullivan's party I was reliving that tackle in my mind as I watched Dave place his hand on Chelsey's lower back and flirt with her right in front of me. We'd won the game against Westfield, so at least Coach was happy with me again.

It was funny how when someone's parents were out of town, it didn't matter if you were friends with them at school or not, everyone was here. I saw Zoey's friend Morgan, and I scanned the room looking for her, but she didn't seem to be here. Chelsey walked over to where I was standing in the kitchen.

She walked her manicured fingers up my chest. "Hey, Matty," she said, drawing out my name. "I saw what you did for me on the field today."

"I didn't do that for you." I looked straight ahead, over her head.

"You wanted to fight Dave for my honor, and I think that's sweet." She pulled her lip gloss from her purse and ran the tube across her already shiny lips.

I hated that stuff, I'd get all sticky when we kissed and smell like watermelon for hours afterward. I hated watermelon. She wasn't listening to me at all. "Chels—I broke up with you, remember?"

She looked up meeting my eyes for the first time. "Why did you break up with me?" She pouted, pushing her lips out, looking ridiculous.

I couldn't even explain it to myself, let alone to her. Sure, the captain of the football team was supposed to date the captain of the cheerleading squad. But I don't know, I couldn't pretend to be that perfect guy anymore. Little by little he was slipping away from me. I was cracking. She was still looking up at me, waiting for me to answer. "I just needed some space."

"Well, if you ever get lonely." She placed her hand against my chest. I was glad I'd benched today. Let her feel what she wasn't going to have.

I turned and walked away. I sat down on a couch and rubbed my temples. The annoying hip hop song blaring from the speakers was giving me a headache. Two sophomore girls I vaguely recognized from school came and sat on either side of me. "Hi, Matt," the blonde said. "I'm Lindsay. And this is Sara." She nodded towards the brunette girl on my other side.

"Enjoying the party?" I asked. They each scooted in toward me.

"It's okay," Lindsay said. She started playing with my hair, rubbing her hand down the back of my neck.

Sara ran her hand up my arm under the sleeve of my T-shirt. It sent a shiver through me, and coupled with the way her friend was tickling my neck it should have felt pretty nice, so why couldn't I loosen up and enjoy the attention? I took a deep breath and looked around the room. Everything was happening around me while I floated above it all, disconnected. The glazed over looks on my teammates faces, the group in the kitchen taking body shots of

Bree Hohman's stomach. They all seemed so damn happy and suddenly I couldn't take it anymore. I had to get out of there.

I got up and extracted myself from their hands. "I've gotta go." *Man, I was stupid.* I headed out to my truck without saying goodbye to anyone. I didn't want anyone trying to talk me out of leaving or making me feel weird for leaving now, just when the horny underclassmen were ready to undress me.

I drove in silence, not even wanting the sound of the radio invading my space.

My parents were asleep when I got home. I grabbed a cold slice of pizza from the fridge and headed back to my room. I passed the picture of John in the hall every day, but for some reason tonight I stopped in front of it and roughly swallowed down the bite of pizza.

I looked at his face and wondered why he couldn't have smiled in the picture. He was in his blue dress Marine uniform, his white cap pulled low with a serious expression on his face. If you knew John, you would've understood how out of place that expression looked on his face. He was always smiling, flashing his dazzling white teeth at friends and strangers alike.

I ran my hand over my newly buzzed hair. I told myself I'd shaved it off so I wouldn't have to style it, but I knew the real reason was so that I'd look more like him. I ran my hand across my head again and again, feeling the prickly hair against my palm. When I glanced in the mirror, or walked past a window, it was like he was back here with me, if only for the briefest of moments.

My parents never talked about him anymore. I felt like I couldn't even say his name around them, and I hated them for that – for taking that last bit of him away from me. I went to my room and threw the uneaten pizza into the trash can under my desk. I sat down at my desk and flipped open my notebook. It opened to the list I'd made with Zoey today. I turned the page over and started writing.

I'm going to Paris

With a girl named Zoey

I don't know what to think about my life anymore

Football. Parties. Practice. Parents. It all feels fake

My jaw hurts from smiling

I want to feel again, I want to live

But instead I turn my head the other way

I crumpled up the piece of paper and threw it into the trash. I rested my head in my hands and brushed repeatedly over my hair. It was becoming a habit.

John's death left a huge hole inside me. And the almost daily headaches made it hard to forget. I never used to get them before. There were two distinct parts to my life—me before his death and the me he left behind after. They felt like two separate people. He'd died from a gunshot wound to the head, and I knew it was twisted, but whenever my head started throbbing, I thought about how it must have felt for him to die. No one knew about the headaches, and to all outside spectators I was still Matt, maintaining a reputable B average, captain of the four and one football team and boyfriend to the most popular girl in school, well until yesterday.

I was careful not to do anything that would cause my parents to worry. I knew my mom couldn't handle anything more, so I played the role expected of me, the son she needed me to be. I couldn't fall apart, that was her job. And for the last four months, I tried to be the perfect boyfriend too, but now I couldn't keep up the effort, especially with Chelsey—that girl was seriously high maintenance. She started off as a good distraction, but then it became just another act I had to keep up with and it all became too much. My headaches had gotten more intense and I couldn't pretend with her anymore.

It had taken everything in me to maintain the picture-perfect status I'd worked so hard to achieve. On the outside, you'd never know that I barely knew how to live in a world where my brother didn't exist.

John hadn't lived at home for the last two years of his life. First, he'd tried college, but flunked out after realizing getting trashed and inflicting pregnancy scares weren't on the curriculum at all. Then he'd joined the Marines and was sent to Afghanistan. I'd only seen him a dozen or so times in these past two years, so why did it like part of me was gone? A part I'd never get back.

I looked out my open door into John's old room. The room my mother had turned into a generic-looking guest room six months ago, just months after his death. There was a suitcase on the floor, and I figured my mom had started packing for me. I walked across the hall and flipped on the light. The room had even been repainted stark-white. It didn't smell like him anymore.

I found all my clothes for the trip folded in neat piles on his old bed. I opened the black roller suitcase on the floor and started putting everything inside. Eight pairs of boxers neatly folded, eight pairs of socks rolled together, white undershirts, jeans, a pair of khaki's, which I almost tossed aside, then decided to keep, in case we went somewhere nice. There was a Frommer's Travel Guide on top of my T-shirts. I flipped through the pages. I knew I should appreciate the things she did for me, but I just wanted to be able to talk—to not be some fucking robot family that acts like nothing's wrong.

Chapter Five

Zoey

I waited for my dad to get home last night, so when my alarm went off at eight, I was still exhausted. I'd reminded my dad about the pre-trip meeting we had this morning. He'd given me a twenty for spending money and said I'd have to go the meeting myself, he doubted he or my mom would be up yet. And he was right.

I was the first one up, but Cora wasn't far behind me. We sat at the table, eating cereal together. "Wanna help me with the laundry today?" I asked, slicing a banana into her Cheerios.

"Sure," she said. She sounded so grown up. I both liked it and didn't.

After breakfast we packed up my dad's car with six laundry baskets in the trunk and backseat and headed over to S&J's Laundromat. I'd pretty much spent every Sunday here since I was thirteen. Only now, I wouldn't be here this Sunday—I'd be in Paris, responsible for no one but myself. I could hardly wait.

Cora helped by carrying in the laundry detergent and the bag of quarters while I heaved the baskets inside. We commandeered three commercial-sized washers in the front and I stuffed the clothes inside while she used the step stool and filled them with quarters. The commercial washers were more expensive, but not twice as much as the regular washers, so it was still cheaper to do giant loads in these rather than use six separate machines. I mixed all the colors together with reckless abandon. No wonder most of our clothes came out looking grayish.

"Excuse me, but you might consider separating your whites," a male voice said behind me.

Without looking behind me I replied, "Yeah, and when you're down to wearing bathing suit bottoms because you're out of underwear, you do it this way." I stood up and turned, suddenly face to face with Matt Parker. *Awesome.* "What are you doing here?" I straightened my shoulders and pushed my hair out of my face.

"You mean other than blushing at your total lack of a filter?" I narrowed my eyes. "Picking up a quilt my mom had cleaned." He moved past me to the service counter. But not before glancing back at me in a way that made me shudder. He was picturing me in my bikini bottoms. *Weirdo.*

"Come on, Cora, we have twenty-three minutes to enjoy ourselves in the lovely confines of the Laundromat waiting room." She followed behind me and picked up an old coloring book from the kid's table.

"Got any crayons, Zoey?" she asked, looking up at me.

"I think I have a pen in my purse." I offered it to her while watching Matt collect the white fluffy down comforter from the counter. He tipped his head at me before walking out into the sunshine.

I flipped open my Calculus book to look at next week's assignment. Just because some of us would be missing school for the class trip, didn't mean we didn't have to keep up on the homework assignments while we were gone. I hoped to get ahead before I left, rather than trying to cram it all in when I was jetlagged. My phone buzzed in my bag, and Cora handed it to me. I fished the phone out from the bottom of my purse.

"Hello?"

"Hey, Zoey." It was Morgan. I hadn't even bothered to check the caller ID, she was pretty much the only person who called me.

"Hey, Morgan. How was Brandon's last night?"

"Ah—mazing. Everyone was there. That sucked you couldn't come. Is Pete okay?" she asked.

"Oh, yeah. We got him through it. That reminds me though, his inhaler's still at school," I said to myself more than to her. "Oh, guess what? Jordan came by last night."

"What? After the party? He did disappear early."

I turned away from Cora. "Yeah, he was looking for some sweet, sweet lovin'."

"Yeah, and how'd that work out for him?" I could tell she was smirking.

"I let him down gently, Morgan, you know me." I glanced back to check on Cora. She was still coloring with my black pen.

"I do know you—too well, Zoey. Anytime a guy gets interested in you, you find a way to back out of it."

"Not true."

"Umm, true and you know it. What's wrong with Jordan? You seemed to like him just fine last weekend—that is before he started liking you. You always have to be in control, Zoey. I'm not saying it's bad, it's just how you are. You never let anyone get close."

I was silent on the other end.

"I mean look at me and you—we're best friends, but I've never even been inside your house."

I guess she had noticed that. I sighed. "Are we done?"

"We're done. Next topic," she said. "What are you doin' later?"

"At the Laundromat right now. I have a meeting in a Mr. Rhinehart's classroom little bit. Ugh, and get this—I'm paired with Matt Parker for the assignment in Paris."

"Yeah, that sounds horrible," she mocked. "He's a hottie."

I couldn't believe what I was hearing. Sure Morgan easily floated between the social circles at school and didn't really belong in any one group over another, but even she should realize that goody-two-shoes jock-boy and I had nothing in common.

"Morgan," I sighed, shaking my head. My voice sounded tired.

"You need to loosen up. Have fun—hook up with the star football player in Paris, whatever, Zoey. Just stop being all dramatic. This is all good stuff —you're freakin going to Paris for a week and you got paired with a hot guy. Who'd you want, Albert Price?" she joked.

Albie was the laughing stock of the school. He was ninety-eight pounds tops, and insisted on wearing sweatpants to school and talked incessantly about bacon to anyone who would listen. I didn't mean to, but I started laughing.

Morgan joined me. "There, that's better," she said.

"Yeah, I guess so."

Cora tapped on my knee. "Our machines are done," she said, pointing to our washers.

I nodded to her. "I gotta go. See ya, Morgan."

Chapter Six

Matt

The only reason I wasn't working at my parent's store this Saturday was because I agreed to run my mom's errands before I left for the trip. So far this morning I'd been to the dry cleaners, pharmacy, post office and then to the Laundromat where I'd had an awkward run-in with Zoey.

I carried everything inside, set my mom's pills on the counter then pulled open the fridge. I started blankly inside and thought about the way Zoey looked bent over, cramming a mountain of laundry into a washer. Their washer at home must have been broken, because she was doing enough laundry to last a month. I stood up and let the fridge swing closed.

I went to my room and organized my papers for the trip one last time. I had my passport, an envelope with important phone numbers and some money, my immunization records and some other stuff my mom stuffed in. Our trip itinerary sat folded on the top of the pile.

My phone chirped from the other room and I jogged to grab it. It was Justin. "Hey man, what's up?"

"You have time for a B-ball game later? We're meeting up at Bryant Park," Justin said.

I glanced at the clock. "Yeah, what time?"

"Three."

"Cool—see you there." I clicked the phone off and headed out to pick up my mom for the pre-trip meeting.

Everyone else had one parent with them, but I was flanked by both my mom and dad in the front row of the classroom. Mr. Rhinehart passed out a sheet of paper to each parent with the phone number to his international cell, his email address, and a detailed day-by-day itinerary. He stopped in front of Zoey's desk and pressed his lips together. "Where's your parent?" he asked.

She shrugged. "They couldn't make it," she said.

"Zoey." He released a deep sigh, that hissed through his teeth and all heads in the room turned to watch their exchange. "Somehow this doesn't surprise me. Did you even tell them?" he asked.

She pushed her shoulders back and looked straight up at him. "Of course I told them. They. Couldn't. Come," she said, enunciating each word.

He gripped the papers tighter in his hands. "Well, no parents, no trip." He stepped passed her desk and handed a flyer to Jared's mom, seated behind her.

Zoey stood up suddenly, bumping against the top of the desk. "What the hell? You can't do that!" She took the papers from his hands. "Just give me one. I'll give it to my dad when I get home."

He pulled the papers back from her. "It's not that easy. I always talk with the parents before this trip, calm their worries and explain the itinerary."

Zoey continued looking straight at Mr. Rhinehart. "Well, trust me, my parents won't be worried and they'd probably instantly lose the paper you gave them."

Mr. Rhinehart shifted his weight. "Zoey, this isn't up for discussion. Go home, get a parent and come back." All eyes were on them now and he knew it. He continued past Zoey, passing out the papers. Zoey seemed indifferent. She stood watching him hand out the papers, then hurried to keep up with him.

"This is bullshit. You can't do this—you can't take this away from me. I did all the fundraising, I paid for everything." She actually looked nervous, something I'd never seen on her. She took a deep breath. "I don't think you understand—my parents aren't going to come."

He studied her for a minute and nodded. "Sit down, Zoey. We'll talk after."

She returned to her desk and sat down, looking bored.

The hour passed with Mr. Rhinehart droning on about travel tips. I couldn't help glancing back at Zoey, trying to figure out why she said her parent's wouldn't come. I caught only bits of what Mr. Rhinehart was saying…money belts, generally safe, but pickpockets in touristy areas, electrical socket adapters, exchanging money.

He clapped his hands together, pulling my attention back to the front. "And that's pretty much it. Our meet-up place at the airport will be in front of the Air France ticket counter at seven fifteen."

Zoey was the first one out of the room. I smirked when I saw Mr. Rhinehart's face turn red. She must've forgotten he told her to stay after. Maybe I'd be doing the assignment by myself after all.

*****

A few minutes before three, I parked and got out of my truck, basketball tucked under my arm and walked up to join the guys who were messing around on the court.

"Mat-ty," Justin called, tossing a ball straight for my head. I ducked at the last second rather than catching it so he'd have to jog after it. "Dick," he jogged past me.

I rolled the extra ball I was holding to the sidelines and joined the guys on the court to pick teams. Bryce, Jake and Conner were on the South Lake basketball team and Tim was on the JV football team.

"Hey bro, those sophomore girls were mackin' last night, why'd you leave?" Justin asked, jogging back up.

Of course he noticed that. The other guys looked at me, waiting to hear my answer. "Yeah, I had to go."

"Well, let's just say you missed out. Someone had a happy ending at the end of the night." He smiled.

"Good for you." I shoved the ball into his chest.

We divided into teams, and I landed with Jake and Conner. I didn't want to be on Justin's team anyway —that way I could check him with an elbow to the ribs for throwing that ball at me.

"We're skins," Bryce said, pulling his shirt over his head. Tim tossed the ball at him and he easily plucked it from the air, showing off, dribbling between his legs. Bryce and I went to the free-throw line and each took a shot to see which team got the ball first.

We both missed our first shot, but Bryce sunk the second one and Justin jogged after it to get the rebound. He palmed the ball

Eliza Jane

and dribbled once, forcing it under his leg, then headed down the court with it.

He took a shot and missed.

I jumped and grabbed the ball, holding it to my side while Bryce and Justin swarmed me. I ducked to the side to get away from them, and dribbled out to center court, giving myself more space. And then suddenly, Bryce was on me, when I went right, he went right, and when I went left, so did he. I had no shot, so I dribbled out to center court, trying to get some room. I watched his foot work, trying to predict which way he'd go next and guessed right. He shifted on the balls of his feet and I sprung past him to take a shot. I missed.

We played for a little while longer, then took a break on the benches once it was tied twenty-one, twenty-one. I swigged from a bottle of Gatorade and wiped the sweat off my forehead with the sleeve of my T-shirt. The afternoon sun was glaring down on us.

"Look at those jackasses." Justin pointed at the group of skaters over at the skate park. We glanced over at the half-pipe and a few small rails—our town's attempt at being hip. It was mostly frequented by the stoners and their girlfriends. "Hey, Matt, isn't that Zoey Marshall, your Parisian lover?"

I glanced over and saw Zoey sitting cross-legged in the grass watching the guys skate. "F-off, Justin." I shoved him from the end of the bench.

42

"You tapping that?" Bryce asked.

"Uh, no." I shook my head. I looked over at Zoey again. She was watching Jordan on the half-pipe. I wondered after what happened in Rhinehart's class if she'd be at the airport in the morning.

Chapter Seven

Zoey

"Damn, Matt Parker looks like sex on a stick," Morgan said, shielding her eyes from the sun. I followed her gaze across the park and watched him get out of his SUV and walk towards the basketball courts. He was wearing mesh shorts and a faded black Interpol T-shirt. So maybe his taste in music wasn't completely tragic. "Zoey, are you looking?" She elbowed me in the side without taking her eyes from him.

"I see him," I said. He ducked and a ball sailed over his head.

"Did you see that, babe?" Jordan asked, calling my attention back to him. He was standing beside the rail he'd been trying to grind on, and failing at, all afternoon.

"Sorry, I missed it," I said.

He glanced over and caught onto what we'd been looking at. A few of the guys had now stripped off their shirts, but to my disappointment, Matt wasn't one of them. Jordan walked over to us and sat down, taking a swig of my Diet Coke.

"What've they got that I don't?" he asked, puffing out his chest.

Morgan looked him over with an eye brow raised, her mouth quirked up. "Let's see, for starters, pectorals, trimmed nose hair, actual athleticism…"

"Nevermind." Jordan held up his hand in front of her face. He pulled a cigarette out of his pocket and lit it, then blew the smoke in Morgan's direction.

She waved a hand in front of her face, clearing the puff of smoke, then took the cigarette from him and took a drag. "Zoey's gonna get with that." She pointed at Matt with the cigarette.

I rolled my eyes. Morgan was seriously delusional sometimes. "I'm going—I've still gotta pack," I said, standing up and dusting the grass from my jeans. I left them with Jordan glancing between Matt and his own flexed bicep with a confused look on his face. I looked over once more to see Matt take a shot and miss. Guess he wasn't so lucky after all.

*****

After stuffing most of what I owned into our ratty black suitcase, I sat down at my desk and wrote out a detailed itinerary of that week's household routine. Ty had band practice after soccer on

Tuesdays and wasn't home until nine, Cora had swim lessons on Wednesday, Charlie should play outside, not sit in front of his video games after school and Pete needed reminders about studying his spelling words and had a diorama due on Thursday for social studies. Charlie needed a refill on his ADD meds and needed to have his paper on Egypt finished by Thursday, since he was giving an oral book report on Friday, and there were parent-teacher conferences at the middle school on Tuesday night. The chances of all of this being accomplished with me gone were slim to none. I tried not to think about that as I jogged down the stairs to start the macaroni and cheese for dinner.

Chapter Eight

Matt

We pulled up to the airport, and I assumed I'd just jump out at the curb, but my dad pulled into the covered ramp and took twenty minutes finding a spot to park just so they could walk me inside. It was already almost 7:20 and I hoped the group was still waiting by the Air France counter.

We were about to walk through the sliding doors into the airport when a commotion at the curbside drop-off caught my attention. Zoey was being accosted by a little girl—the same one that had been with her at the Laundromat.

Zoey dropped down on her knees, smoothing the little girl's wild hair back from her face and talked to her in a low voice I couldn't understand. She stood up and handed her dad a sheet of paper, which he folded and tucked into his back pocket. They looked like they were arguing about something, and when I got closer, I heard Zoey say something about staying home.

"Pete's got a diorama due and Charlie's got a book report, and Mom… I shouldn't even be going."

Her dad shook his head and handed her her backpack. "We'll manage, Zoe—you need to go."

Zoey looked unsure, but shrugged into her backpack. "Dad, don't forget Pete's inhaler's almost out of juice."

"We'll get it refilled. Stop worrying and go enjoy yourself."

The little girl was still crying and wrapped herself tighter around Zoey's legs. And at that exact moment, the wheels of my suitcase jammed against the uneven sidewalk, pulling Zoey's attention over to me. She wiped her eyes with the back of her hand, and quickly looked away. She gave the little girl one last kiss and strode through the doors ahead of me without a single glance back.

Unfortunately my parents were still following me. They were so freakin embarrassing sometimes. I saw the group up ahead by the counter, and walked ahead of my parents. It was time for my mom to cut the cord. Zoey got there a second before I did. I wondered if Mr. Rhinehart would give her a hard time for yesterday, but he seemed particularly jolly for a Sunday morning. It was exceptionally impressive given that the day ahead of us would involve two planes and sixteen hours total travel time until we landed in Paris. My mom talked to Mr. Rhinehart for a second, then gave me a hug. My dad shook my hand and told me to be careful, and they turned to leave, thank God.

After getting through security, our group spent the hour and a half waiting to board by lounging around in the seating area we'd taken over. A group of kids went off to get their last fix of American fast food for a week, but I pulled my cap low on my head and listened to music until it was finally time to board.

I slid in to the window seat, scooting my way around Cho, the mathlete, and Zoey who was in the middle. I pulled out my iPod and shuffled through until I found the Zen-like playlist I'd created for the flight. I didn't particularly like flying and thought this might help. Plus, I didn't want to find out if the altitude would play havoc on my headaches.

I pulled open the window shade and leaned my head against the cool glass, watching the crew load suitcases into the belly of the plane. I was about to pop in my ear buds when I heard Zoey drawing deep breaths next to me. I looked over and saw her eyes were closed and her chest rising and falling systemically. She was sucking air in through her mouth and blowing it out through her nose.

"Stare, much?" she asked, catching me.

I stuck one ear bud in, leaving the other dangling. "Sorry, I just… You don't like flying, huh?"

"What gave you that idea?"

"It's okay, I'm not particularly fond of it either," I admitted.

Then she swallowed and when she spoke again, her voice

was softer. "No, it's just I've actually never been on a plane before."

I watched her for a second to be sure she wasn't messing with me, but she seemed to be telling the truth. "In that case—you should switch seats with me." Her eyebrow shot up, looking confused. "It's definitely better to be able to see what's going on, trust me. It helps you feel more in control." I unbuckled my seat belt. "Come on, take the window seat." I half stood in front of my seat. If she didn't get up soon I was going to look like an idiot crouched here for no reason.

She unbuckled her seat belt and we awkwardly scooted around each other, trading places in the cramped space between the seats. I felt my crotch rub up against her back, but pretended not to notice.

I watched Zoey look out the window and take stock of our surroundings. We were just over the wing, so it somewhat blocked our view, but we could still see that the crew was just about finished loading the belly of the plane with suitcases. Zoey looked back at me and lifted one corner of her mouth. I think it was supposed to be a smile, but it wasn't something I was used to seeing on her, so it was hard to say.

"It's okay to be afraid of flying," I said. "Lots of people are." I dug through my bag and took out a pack of cinnamon gum. "Gum?" I held the pack out to her. She shook her head.

"I'm not afraid of flying," she said.

I made a point of looking down at her hands gripping the ends of the arm rests. She relaxed her fingers and moved her hands to her lap. When was she going to drop this tough girl act? "Here." I held the gum out to her. "Your ears will probably pop when we take off. Chewing gum helps."

She looked at me suspiciously, but took a stick. She unwrapped it but inspected the gum carefully before folding it into her mouth. Did she think I was trying to poison her?

"Why are you being so nice to me?" she asked.

"Hmm?" I asked, chomping down on my own stick. "How am I supposed to act? We're partners, right?"

She stopped chewing and looked directly at me. Her eyes were the softest shade of blue, with hints of gray around the edges. "Yeah, I guess," she said. She resumed chewing her gum. Why was I watching her mouth? I looked back up at her eyes. I could tell she was getting creeped out by me. I turned to face forward. "I just figured you're probably used to people catering to you—you're Matt Parker," she finished.

"And you're Zoey Marshall," I said slowly, unsure of where this was going, but she didn't elaborate. "I was just trying to help. I don't really like flying either."

Instead of answering, she turned her head to look out the window and tuned me out. I put in my headphones and leaned back, closing my eyes to relax to the sounds of gongs and chimes. Man, this was going to be a long week.

Chapter Nine

Zoey

When we reached our cruising altitude, I leaned back from the window and relaxed into my seat. It was both terrifying and kinda cool watching the takeoff. My stomach felt jittery and my ears had popped, just like Matt had said.

I'd settled into my calculus homework for the next hour or so until I was pretty sleepy. But bonus, I had finished all the problems in chapter seven. I stretched and tried to get more comfortable, but settled for leaning my cheek against the window, even though it was straining my neck. What I wouldn't give for one of those little neck pillows I'd seen Amanda Hughes with.

And while I was on the topic of Amanda Hughes, I guess now was as good a time as any to finally face the fact that I was rooming with her in the hotel. I'd ignored her all semester, even after we found out we'd be sharing a room. I could tell she wanted to talk about everything and coordinate outfits and toiletries before we left, but I kept blowing her off and disappearing from class as soon as the bell rang. And thankfully now I was sitting three rows behind her. She wasn't that bad, just abnormally perky for someone with such a smushed in face. I didn't know what she had to be so freakin happy about. I closed my eyes and hoped to get some sleep to pass a few hours of this flight.

*****

When I woke up, my mouth was all dried out from hanging open. I swallowed and opened my eyes, wondering how much time had passed. My head was resting on Matt's shoulder. *Crap!*

I sat up in my own seat. Maybe he was sleeping too and didn't notice. Nope, he was definitely awake. And now he was looking at me.

"Sorry. I fell asleep I guess."

"It's fine."

"How long was I out?"

"Um, about an hour, I guess," he said, glancing down at his watch.

"You could've just shoved me off you," I said.

"It wasn't bothering me," he said, glancing over at me.

Our eyes met momentarily, and it felt too intimate in the close confines. We both looked away. Outside the window, the sun was bright in the sky, so I was probably sleeping longer than an hour.

He'd been writing in his notebook, holding it close to his lap rather than pulling down the little fold down tray, like he didn't want anyone to see what he was writing. He closed the notebook and tucked it in the seat pocket. My eyes lingered on his hands. His nails were clean and trimmed, his fingers long and slender. I blinked away the sleep in my eyes and straightened up.

"So now that you're up, should we talk about our paper?" he asked.

"Uh, sure."

He reached for the notebook again and flipped to the page of notes we'd started together in class. He tilted it towards me. "Any of these sound good to you?" he asked.

I read over the list again, running my finger across the page. Nothing was standing out to me. "Yeah, I still have no ideas."

He slid the notebook book from me and we sat in silence for a few seconds. "What did you mean before when you said I was 'Matt Parker'?" he asked, using air quotes.

He'd picked up on that, huh? Maybe he wasn't quite the dense meathead I always made him out to be. "Don't tell me you don't notice the prostitute-pack that follows you around. Not to mention the teachers cutting you a break and a good portion of the school idolizing you."

He wrinkled his brows. "That stuff doesn't really matter to me," he said, shifting in his seat.

"I doubt that."

"You really don't know me, Zoey."

"I know you're captain of the football team."

"And the wrestling team," he added.

"And your friend Justin is a horny little toad."

"No argument there." He smirked. "But how's that any better than you dating that stoner, Jordan?"

"I'm not dating him," I nearly snorted. "High school relationships are stupid. Sorry, no offense for whatever it is that you and Chelsey have going on." I glanced over at him.

"No—we're not together anymore."

Hm. So I guess that rumors about her cheating on him were true. That must have been a blow to his ego. She was the most lusted after girl in school. Perky, blonde and thin. I'd never actually talked to her. Last week, I'd seen his friend Justin humping his locker after she passed by in the hall, which was not an uncommon reaction on the days she wore her cheerleading uniform to school.

"So what you're trying to say is that there's more to you than playing football with your Neanderthal friends?" I asked.

"Some days I wish there wasn't." He rubbed his hand across his hair several times, looking deep in thought. I spent more time than I'd like to admit analyzing his comment and wondering what it might mean.

"Is there more to you than trying to be invisible at school?" he asked, pulling me from my thoughts. "What are your hobbies?"

"Hobbies?" I scoffed.

"Yeah, those things you do in your free time," he clarified.

I had to really concentrate to come up with something. "Well, if I get the time I guess I like drawing or maybe taking a bath."

"Seriously?" His face was slack.

I rolled my eyes.

"Wow, sounds exciting."

I didn't know why I even bothered trying to talk to him. We didn't say anything else to each other for the rest of the flight.

We landed in New Jersey for our layover and to change planes. I reluctantly succumbed to Amanda's advances and had lunch with her at an overpriced Chinese place in the airport food court.

She whipped out her itinerary and lined up her multi-colored highlighters in the center of the table between us, talking excitedly while I concentrated on my fried rice. I watched her shuffle through the pages of research that she'd cross-referenced against the itinerary and the outline for her paper. It looked like maybe Matt was going to be more low-key to hang out with than I'd first assumed.

She stopped talking and was looking at me expectantly. I swallowed down a bite of egg roll. "Listen, Amanda—I'll probably just be with Matt most of the time. We haven't even figured out what our paper's on yet."

"Oh." She looked down and twirled her spork in her chow mein noodles.

*****

On the flight to Paris I sat in between a middle aged man and woman near the back of the plane. Matt was seven rows in front of me. I could see the top of his head poking above all the others. He had the window seat this time, and now I didn't feel so bad that I'd taken it from him on our last flight. I fished the stick of gum he'd given me right before we boarded from my pocket and settled back for the long flight over the Atlantic.

Chapter Ten

Matt

After landing and getting our luggage, we got into a shuttle for the thirty minute drive into the city of Paris. My head throbbed and between the happy chatter of my classmates and the driver's swerving, the only thing I concentrated on was not getting sick as we barreled down the highway into the city.

I opened my eyes when the van came to its final stop. Our hotel was a simple nine-story pale stone building with an arched front door, awnings over the windows and a dark wooden floor in the lobby. Mr. Rhinehart reminded us we had a few hours to rest in the hotel, or sight see nearby before a trip to the National Museum of History and then a group dinner tonight.

After a quick check-in process, Bobby and I found our room. It was a tiny corner room with two narrow beds, a wardrobe and a flat screen TV mounted on the wall. The tall window billowed with white sheer curtains. I face-planted onto the bed near the window, not even bothering to remove my shoes.

"So I'm gonna go out for a bit," Bobby said.

I grunted and waved one hand blindly over my head, hoping he understood that meant, 'cool see ya later.'"

I heard the door open and sounds of laughter and talking as Bobby met up with the others out in the hall.

*****

The pounding in my head intensified and pulled me from sleep. I cracked one eye open and multi-colored lights flashed before my eyes, even after I closed them again. Sometimes sleeping helped me to get rid of a headache, but not today. The flight and jet lag must have been a perfect combination for a migraine. I realized the pounding wasn't coming from inside my head, but instead against the door. Bobby must have forgotten his key. I got up and stumbled for the door, opened it and then fell back onto the bed.

"Um, hello?"

I looked up and saw Zoey standing in the open doorway. The light flooding in from the hall created a halo around her. "Shut the door," I said into my pillow. I heard the door click softly and was grateful.

"Come on, everyone's going to the museum."

I didn't move.

"What the big, strong, Matt Parker is too jet-lagged to go out?"

I groaned and rolled over onto my side into the fetal position.

"What's wrong?" she asked, her voice softer than before.

"Migraine," I replied without opening my eyes.

"Oh." She hesitated for a second. "Anything I can do?"

"My meds. They're in my bag." I motioned to the suitcase I'd dropped at the end of my bed. I heard her come closer and opened my eyes to watch her crouch down and unzip my suitcase. She carefully moved my boxers aside and dug in between the stacks of T-shirts until she found the pill bottle.

"Is this it?"

I nodded and held out my hand. "Thanks." I squeezed my hand around the bottle and let my hand hang limply off the bed, working up the energy to actually open it.

"Do you need me to get you some water or something?"

"That would be awesome," I whispered.

She pushed my shoulders back until I was lying against the pillow. "Just try and relax. I'll be right back."

A few minutes passed and Zoey knocked softly on the door. I pulled myself out of bed to go open it. I stood there, steadying myself against the door frame, squinting into the light. She put her arm around my waist and guided me back to the bed. I sat down, leaning against the headboard for support. She opened the pill the bottle and handed me one, then brought the opened bottle of water to my lips. I closed my eyes and swallowed the pill down. I didn't know what caused the sudden change in Zoey, or why she was being nice, but I wasn't about to complain right now.

"Thanks, Zoey." I leaned my head back and closed my eyes again.

"Anytime."

"I guess you have to go now," I said, not meeting her eyes.

"I can't just leave you here alone."

I was quiet, trying to figure out what she meant.

"I already told Mr. Rhinehart that you weren't feeling well and that we'd meet up with everyone later But if you don't want me here, I could probably still catch up with them."

I opened my eyes again. Zoey was sitting next to me on the bed, her blue eyes full of concern. "I want you to stay," I said softly.

"Okay then." She stood up and moved to the end of the bed and removed my shoes and set them neatly beside my suitcase.

I scooted down on the bed and laid my head against the pillow. I felt like shit, my neck was stiff, my palms were cold and sweaty and I was nauseous. I really hoped I wouldn't get sick in front of her. She sat down across from me on Bobby's bed and looked at me. "Thanks for taking care of me," I said.

"It's okay, I'm used to it."

I didn't have the brain capacity to try and interpret what that meant. Instead, I concentrated on my breathing, but the room continued to spin, and while headaches normally helped me feel closer to John, I just felt alone and really far from home.

I knew she wasn't the type to worry about keeping up appearances, so I knew she wouldn't judge me for letting my guard down right now and so I did. "Zoey?" I said without opening my eyes.

"Yeah?" she whispered.

"Can you come lay with me?"

She hesitated.

"Please. I think it will help." I reached a hand out towards her.

I felt the bed shift as she sat down next to me on the narrow mattress and reluctantly lay down next to me. She kept her body rigidly balanced on the edge of the bed, so that we weren't touching, but after a few seconds, I inched in closer.

Eliza Jane

The second I felt her against me, an easy calmness washed over me. I curled my body around hers and felt grounded by the way our chests rose and fell together, stopping the room from spinning. It should have felt strange to be lying here with Zoey Marshall, but the thing that worried me the most was that it didn't.

Chapter Eleven

Zoey

Well that was the strangest two hours I'd ever spent—in Matt's arms in a hotel room in Paris. Just wait until Morgan heard this story. There was nothing sexual about it—it had been like taking care of one of my brothers. Lord knows Charlie had asked me to sleep in his room countless times when we were growing up. He had an intense fear of monsters all of second grade. That's all this was, Matt at his weakest, although I was a little surprised he'd let me see him at his most vulnerable.

I'd gone into Mom-mode, nothing more. At least I'd felt useful for the first time on this trip. I wasn't used to only being responsible for myself. And I did kind of like it when he closed his eyes while I raked my fingers through his hair to massage his scalp.

He'd woken up in a completely different state—bright eyed and ready to go see the city. He kept apologizing about making me miss our first excursion of the day, but I honestly didn't care that much. After we checked into the hotel, I'd taken off on my own to get away from Amanda and walked up and down the block our hotel was one. The fear of getting lost kept me from going too far, but I'd sat down beside a fountain and became enamored with the details of this place that felt so completely different than anything at home. Cocky pink-footed pigeons danced at my feet, and people everyone were effortlessly cool in tailored shirts and trim-fit jeans. Paris had a coolness factor, an air to it that dared you to try and become a Parisian. The charming shops along the uneven cobblestone street bore names like Brasserie, Patisserie. And there were sidewalk cafés galore where people lingered over bottles of wine, cigarettes and conversations that sounded all the more fascinating spoken in their accented French.

By the time I made it back to the hotel lobby to meet up with Mr. Rhinehart and the group, my feet were sore and the jet lag had caught up with me. I didn't even notice Matt wasn't around until Mr. Rhinehart told me to go round up my partner.

Even though Paris, so far, was exceeding my expectations, I'd felt sort of useless wandering around the street without a purpose. But when Matt needed me, I felt that familiar pull of being needed and too easily folded myself into his arms.

I thought things might be a little strange between us once we woke up and dislodged ourselves from each other's limbs, but strangely it wasn't. We both wanted to get cleaned up from the flight and change before we met everyone for dinner, so I'd gone to my room to shower while he did the same.

I dried my hair with Amanda's tiny blow dryer and put on some mascara. I didn't know why I was making more of an effort then I ever did at home—it wasn't like this was a date or anything—that'd be hilarious. I slipped into my black ballet flats and went down to the lobby to meet Matt. He was waiting at the open front doors wearing a fitted grey sweater and dark jeans. That boy had definitely grown up taking his Flintstone's vitamins. When he saw me, his face lit up. He looked much better than he had earlier, his skin glowed in a healthy way. I walked past him out the front door.

"Well hello to you too," he said behind me, chuckling.

"Ready?" I asked.

"Yeah, do you know where we're going?"

"I think so." I studied the map I'd grabbed from the lobby, and turned heading left on the stone street. We walked in silence, taking in the sights around us. "Listen, if we're going to work together, there's a few things you should know," I said.

He looked over, waiting for me to continue. He needed to understand that the cuddling thing this afternoon was totally out of character and wasn't going to happen again.

"We will not be acting like dumbass tourists wandering around the city, so if you brought your fanny-pack, you're just going to have to leave it in the room. This is a business arrangement; we'll do our research so we can split up the paper, and that's it. I plan to see, Notre Dame, the Sacred Heart Basilica, the Louvre, and of course the Eiffel Tower—you can do whatever you want."

"I'll come with you. Sacred Heart would be cool," he said.

I glanced over at him, surprised he even knew what it was. "Well, I just don't want you to get any strange ideas based on what happened earlier. We will not be hooking up," I finished, waving my finger in his direction.

He chuckled under his breath. "As much as I appreciate your help today, you don't have to worry about that." He seemed a little too smug about things, a fading smile still on his lips. I wasn't sure why, but I was suddenly a little annoyed that he thought it laughable about the idea of us hooking up. Wasn't he the one who asked me to lay with him in bed earlier?

He glanced over at me and the smile on his lips faded away. "God, if you're that worried about us hanging out together, I'll get you a rape whistle." He quickened his pace past me.

"Hey—we're here," I called. I stopped in front of the café. Matt came back, but walked straight past me, to our group seated at clusters of small tables.

I enjoyed the attention from the male server who looked to be in his mid-twenties. He made a production of helping me into my chair and folding my napkin across my lap while serenading me with French words I had no idea the meanings of. Matt and I took the last two seats at the end of the string of tables.

"Feeling better, I see!" Mr. Rhinehart smiled at Matt. He sounded tipsy. I noted the half-empty glass of wine in front of him. "And, Zoey, thanks for looking after him."

I nodded.

A few of the others had glasses of wine in front of them too, and I saw my classmates with new eyes—they weren't just talking excitedly about their trip to the museum—they were buzzed up.

I flipped open my menu and turned the pages, searching for something I recognized. I reached the end of the menu without finding anything in English. I flipped it over to the back cover, but it was blank. No one around me seemed to be struggling with their menus. Maybe I just needed to loosen up and go with the flow, order something adventurous. How bad could that be? I flipped through the pages again and scanned the headings: apéritifs, repas, then read the words underneath, trying to make sense of them. *Poulet sauce forestière ...pates orecchiette. Courgettes...poisons... copeaux de comté.* It was all in French and there were no pictures on the menu, like back home at Applebee's.

The waiter came back and people started placing their orders at the far end of the table. There was nothing worse than fifteen American teenagers butchering the French language. My ears felt like they were going to fall off. I was more than a little embarrassed to be seen with such amateurs. I tried to be inconspicuous as I glanced around the restaurant trying to see what other people had on their plates, but it didn't help. I didn't know these words.

The waiter was behind my shoulder. Quickly scanning the words again, I settled for pointing at the first thing I saw and he leaned over my shoulder and nodded, then scribbled something on his pad of paper.

When our food came, each plate that was set in front of everyone looked better than the next. But my excitement and hunger quickly faded when the waiter set something in front of me that I didn't recognize. There were small bits of diced, stewed peppers and some type of rank meat-paste. I could tell Matt was laughing behind his napkin. He watched me pick through the mess with my fork and attempt a bite. I knew I made a nasty face, like Cora did when she swallowed down cough syrup. I downed half my water and looked longingly at Amanda's plate with a thin, wood-fired pizza bubbling with melted cheese. I'd give my left ovary for a slice. I reached for the bread basket and took the only slice left, the heel.

Matt loaded up his bread plate with pasta and slid it towards me. "I couldn't possibly finish all this. Have some."

It was thick noodles, baby tomatoes and shaved cheese. It looked amazing.

"No thanks, I'm okay." I picked up my fork in a weak attempt and speared a piece of the steaming pile on my plate.

"Come on, I have a weak stomach—I can't watch you eat

that." He pushed the saucer of pasta towards me.

"What is it?" I asked, poking my fork into the soft center of the meat paste on my plate.

He shook his head. "You don't want to know."

Setting my pride aside, I scooted the saucer the rest of the way towards me and dug in. There was a light sauce coating the noodles—it was sweet like white wine and salty at the same time with hints of garlic and black pepper. Matt was still watching me, but I didn't care. I shoveled twirled fork-fulls of pasta into my mouth and soon finished every bite on the plate.

I looked up and Matt was eating his now dwindling plate of pasta. "You want more?" he asked with a noodle dangling from his mouth.

"No thanks, that was really good though."

He nodded and slurped the noodle, causing it to disappear between his lips.

Watching him eat it was the first time I noticed his lips looked really kissable—full and soft. He wiped the napkin across his mouth, breaking my concentration. Morgan had been right about him, and I figured there was nothing wrong with looking.

I wished I was brave enough to order a glass of wine, but after that debacle with ordering my meal, I sipped my water and stayed quiet.

After a leisurely dinner, our group walked back to the hotel, but rather than going inside people took off in small groups after Mr. Rhinehart told us we had an eleven o'clock curfew, but not to go off alone. I didn't feel like spending any more time with my noisy classmates than I already had. I was feeling embarrassed enough that I was American.

I sat down on the edge of a fountain out in front of our hotel. I missed my brothers and sister and wondered how they were faring without me.

"Hey," Matt said behind me.

I pulled my bare feet out of the fountain and turned towards him. "I thought you went off with Bobby and them."

"Naw. I guess I didn't feel like it."

"Oh." He was just standing awkwardly in front of me—I tried not to notice that I was face to face with his crotch. "Do you want to sit down?"

"Actually, I was wondering if you wanted to get some ice cream. You must still be hungry and I saw a place just down the street."

"Uh, sure." I tried to sound cool and nonchalant, but that sounded pretty perfect to me. We walked down the street to tiny store front with a hand painted sign that said *Crème glacée*. It was just big enough instead the store for the glass cooler and old fashioned cash register. Muted colors of creamy frozen goodness stared back at us. I ordered the melon flavor and Matt asked for pistachio.

"Pistachio?" I challenged.

"If I don't order it, who else is going to?" He smirked. He felt bad for the pistachio flavored gelato. My smile faded almost just as quickly. Is that why we were hanging right now, because if he hadn't offered to hang out with me tonight, he knew I'd be alone and he some sort of guilt since I stayed with him today? I didn't need his pity. He stepped up to the counter and paid for both of us, then tipped his cup towards mine. "Cheers."

"You didn't have to pay for me." I hurried out behind him.

"I know. But you bought me a bottle of water earlier, so now we're even."

Well I guess that was fair. No sense making a big deal out of it. We walked back to the hotel, eating our gelato.

"Well, what should we do? Call it a night?" I asked once we reached the hotel lobby.

"We could plan out our topic for the paper," Matt suggested.

"Oh." Had I been delusional thinking that Matt Parker actually wanted to hang out with me?

"Or not." He took a bite and smiled at me.

"I think my roommate Amanda brought some games. I could go up and get a deck of cards or something."

He nodded. "I'll come with you."

When we reached my room, I left him in the open doorway holding both cups of gelato while I rummaged around in the room. I flung my black lace bra from the back of a chair to the other side of my bed, hoping he hadn't seen it. "Cards?" I asked, holding up the deck.

"Or I could teach you how my brother and I used to play this." He picked up a game of Scrabble.

"Scrabble?" My grandparents played Scrabble.

"Come on, you'll like it."

I shrugged and shoved the game under my arm and followed him into the hall.

We set the game up on a small pedestal table in the street outside our hotel, lit only by strings of white Christmas lights that crisscrossed above us. We flipped over all the tiles.

"So you said you play this with your brother?" I asked.

"I used to." He smiled like he was remembering something good. "If you're up for it, the way we used to play was to each take nine tiles, rather than seven like the rules say and you can only spell perverted words." He looked up for my reaction. "We were kinda immature—we don't have to…"

"Are you kidding me? Dirty Scrabble sounds way better than the regular way. Why nine tiles?" I asked.

"John said it made it easier to make better words."

"John's your brother?" I asked.

He nodded, but looked down, suddenly becoming fascinated by his tiles.

"So it's just the two of you, then? No other siblings?"

His fingers stopped rearranging the tiles, but his eyes stayed cast down. "Actually it's just me now. John passed away last year."

"Oh, I'm sorry—I didn't know." My hands felt clumsy on the table, I wanted to reach out and grab his hand, but I was bad at this stuff. I couldn't even imagine losing one of my siblings. They were my whole life.

We just sat in silence for a few seconds, Matt looking down at the table. When he looked up at me, his eyes were watery.

"Let's make some dirty words in John's honor," I said.

He smiled. "Let's."

I picked out nine tiles. They barely fit across the little tray. It was obviously designed to hold seven. After studying his tiles for a minute, Matt went first, laying the word MILF horizontally across the center of the board.

"Can you do that?" I asked.

"Oh yeah, slang, acronyms, anything goes. As long as it's perverted."

"John's rules?" I asked, raising an eyebrow.

He smiled and nodded.

I thought only using dirty words would be harder, but it turns out they came to me more naturally than regular words. I laid down GROIN next.

"Nice. John would be proud." He reached over to refill the tiles on his tray. "So you have a sister, right?"

I remembered that he'd seen Cora and I at the Laundromat. "Yeah. And three little brothers."

"Wow. Big family."

"Yep." My thought exactly—who the hell had five kids nowadays?

He put down CUM next, then I laid down LOAD.

"Good one." He gave me a fist bump across the table.

"So why didn't you want to hang out with those guys tonight?"

He grew quiet and rearranged his tiles. "I don't know, I guess I just feel like I have to pretend to be someone I'm not around a lot of people. They expect me to be happy all the time and I'm just tired of faking it."

I nodded. I understood. I didn't fit most of the time. I knew he was paying me a compliment even without saying it. He didn't have to be fake around me.

"Pussy has two s's, right?" he asked, a look of concentration on his face.

"Last time I checked."

"Can we go with one?" he asked.

"Pu-sy," I tried it out loud. We cracked up laughing. "That doesn't sound right."

"Here." He turned his letter towards me. "Help me." I studied the tiles on his tray, then rearranged them and spelled the word NUDE. "You're good at this." He grinned, and took the tiles to arrange on the board.

"Yeah, I don't know what that says about me," I said, but soaked in his compliment.

Eliza Jane

Chapter Twelve

Matt

By our second morning, I anticipated that Zoey wouldn't be fully functioning until she had her coffee. I got us a table in the small breakfast nook off the hotel lobby, and carried saucers with one of everything over to our table. Chocolate croissants, pastries with sticky orange jam in the center, pale, thin yogurt topped with raisins, and soft cheeses with hunks of baguette. Zoey slid into the seat across from me, her eyes scanning the table. I flipped her coffee cup over just as the waitress came by with a pot of coffee. "Café?" she asked.

"Oui." I held up Zoey's cup. When it was filled with steaming, creamy-frothed coffee, I sat it back down in front of her. She remained speechless as she eyed the coffee.

"Uh, thanks," she recovered, fumbling for the mug.

After breakfast, our group set off on the twenty-minute walk toward Notre Dame. The streets were steep and winding and dotted with stone buildings and shops adorned with awning-covered windows. Bobby and Carson ran ahead of the group, practicing French swear words and cracking up laughing at the combinations they could put together. Like cheese dick. It made me miss the time I spent with just me and Zoey. She was low key, and there was a certain degree of sadness inside her that felt familiar, reliable to me.

Before long, Zoey and I found ourselves several paces behind the group. We walked in silence toward the river and then Notre Dame came into view – its two towers standing tall against the brilliant blue sky.

After rounds of class photos on the stone steps outside, Mr. Rhinehart finally ushered us inside. As soon as we stepped into the dimly lit, soaring cathedral my head tipped back in appreciation. It had an old, magical feel to it. A hushed silence fell over our group. Mr. Rhinehart stepped in line to buy the group rate tickets and secure our audio guides for an English-speaking tour. Although it seemed more like a historic monument than an actual church,

We walked the twenty-minutes to get there, and when we crossed the river and saw its two towers standing against the blue sky, it was way better seeing it in person than in a history book photo.

After Notre Dame, Zoey and I grabbed a quick lunch, eating pizza on a park bench. Apparently here you ordered one pizza per person. Zoey and I each got a tomato basil pizza. She didn't want to take any chances ordering on her own, so she just repeated my order. The pizza was light and thin with a rich tomato sauce and not much chees, and weren't shaped in a perfect circle like back at home, but I appreciated their imperfections. It was delicious.

"Zoey, I just wanted to tell you, last night was cool—it felt really good talking about John like he was still real. I asked Chelsey to play perverted Scrabble with me once before and she wouldn't, she told me to grow up."

"I guess I just like dirty words more than most girls."

"Well thanks anyways."

"Anytime," she said and stuffed the last of the pizza crust into her mouth. As small as she was, the girl could eat.

"So Zoey, tell me something most people don't know about you."

"Why?" she asked around the bite of pizza.

"I don't know, just so we can get to know each other better. I mean we've been going to school together our whole lives, but I don't really know anything about you."

She swallowed down the pizza and stared at me blankly.

"Okay…I'll start." I wiped my mouth. "What do you want to know about me?" I asked.

She studied me and I suddenly felt self-conscious under her gaze. Did I have tomato sauce on my chin? "What did you mean on the plane when you said you wished there wasn't more to your life than football?"

I ran my hand across my hair. "Ah, next question."

She rolled her eyes. "How did your brother die?"

Man, she didn't hold back. "I'd rather talk about him than his death."

She nodded. "Okay, then tell me something about him."

"He was three years older than me and I basically worshipped him growing up. I was like his shadow, but he never got annoyed with it somehow. He was a Marine, and when he came back from basic training he was built. That's when I started working out. I always wanted to be like him, and now that he's not here—it's like I don't know what I'm doing anymore. Since it's been a year everyone expects me to be moved on, and my parents don't even talk about him anymore. Sorry, I don't even know why I'm talking about this—I don't mean to be such a downer."

"I'm not really one for sunshine and rainbows if you haven't noticed."

"You're alright, Zoey Marshall."

"And you're not as bad as I would've guessed." She slugged my shoulder.

"Thanks?"

"Come on, we gotta get back," she said, standing up, brushing crumbs from her lap.

"Hey—you didn't tell me anything about you."

"Just ask me something. What do you want to know?" she asked.

I thought for a second, trying to come up with something that would make her laugh. "Were you really wearing a bikini when I saw you at the Laundromat?"

She glared at me like I was a perv. "That's what you want to know?"

I held up my hands in surrender. "What? I am a guy. I was just curious."

"Well for your information, yes. Bathing suit bottoms can double for underwear in a pinch. I figured it was better than wearing nothing."

I considered it and nodded. I hoped she couldn't tell my neck was turning pink under the collar of my polo.

*****

After the group trip, where I would've appreciated the Zoey method—skipping ahead to see the good stuff, and then another long dinner—where Zoey had me order for her—we were hanging out in the hotel lobby trying to think of what to do with our remaining hours of freedom before the curfew Mr. Rhinehart imposed.

Bobby was trying to convince a group to go down the street to a dance club he was sure would let us in.

"You'll come right?" Bobby asked, looking at me.

I didn't really care, but didn't want people to think I was lame after skipping their group outing last night. "Sure." I looked over at Zoey, sitting alone in the window seat drawing in her sketch pad. "Who's going?" I asked Bobby.

"Just me, you, Amanda and Stephanie. They're upstairs getting dressed." He grinned.

"Should we ask Zoey?" I nodded towards her.

"No. I want tonight to be fun. Plus, there's two of them, two of us. It's perfect."

"I'm gonna ask her—I don't just want to walk out past her without at least inviting her. She probably won't even come." I stood and headed towards her, hoping she would come.

"Big plans tonight?" she asked without looking up when I got closer.

"Come with me." I sat down next to her, trying to see what she'd been drawing, but she moved the book away before I could see what it was.

"Bobby doesn't want me there," she said, closing the book and setting it aside. We looked over at him across the lobby. He scowled back at us.

"Forget Bobby, I want you there."

"Why?" she challenged.

Man this girl didn't take anything you told her without an argument.

"Because I don't want to be the only one faking it around the happy people." I smiled at her. Amanda and Stephanie bounded down the stairs, giggling in tube tops and short skirts, further illustrating my point.

"Oh, I won't be faking anything."

"And that's what I like about you. Come on, Zoey." I pulled her up by her hands. "Go put your book away." She narrowed her eyes at me. "It'll be fun."

We crossed the lobby and headed back to the others. "Zoey's going to come with us," I said.

"Not wearing that, she's not," Stephanie said, wrinkling her nose.

I thought Zoey looked fine in her jeans and T-shirt, but before either Zoey or I knew what was happening, the girls were carting her up the stairs by the elbows.

They emerged fifteen minutes later and I hardly recognized Zoey. She wore a black tank top and a tiny skirt and her long dark hair curled around her bare shoulders. She looked smokin' hot, way better than either Amanda or Stephanie, though they'd probably taken three times as long to get ready. I looked away and re-checked my wallet, counting my money again, even though I knew I had forty-six euros.

We walked about a mile and reached *le Secret*, and paid to get in. We stuck together in an awkward clump by the bar while we scoped things out. After shouting over the music to find out what the girls wanted, Bobby and I returned with drinks. There were two floors with separate music playing, the main floor was more of a lounge and the second floor had loud-thumping dance music with lights and lasers flashing from the ceiling. There were basically two types of people there, tourists like us and sleazy guys trying to pick up the tourists.

Amanda and Stephanie held hands and headed to the dance floor, trying to put on a show. Bobby gawked at them. He wouldn't have had a chance with either of them back home, but that was the funny thing about this trip, you could forge new relationships and be someone different than who you were at home. Bobby joined the girls on the dance floor and left Zoey and I standing together, sipping our drinks.

It was too loud to talk, but I tried anyways. "Having fun?"

She nodded.

I tried again. "Do you like to dance?"

She shrugged.

It wasn't a no. I wanted to say something clever, like 'when in Rome' and grab her hand. But I took a sip of my beer instead. Stephanie headed towards us with a toothy smile. She grabbed my hand. "Come on." And pulled me towards the dance floor. I glanced back at Zoey, but let Stephanie lead me away.

Stephanie swayed her hips in front of me, bumping her hips into mine. I think she meant it to be sexy, but it just seemed forced. I wasn't good at dancing so I settled for shifting my weight from side to side. Stephanie grabbed my hands and put them on her waist. She smiled up at me. I wasn't really feeling this. I looked back to check on Zoey, but she wasn't where I left her. My eyes scanned the room, searching for her. Had she left? I looked around Stephanie's bouncing head and spotted Zoey on the other side of the dance floor being freaked by some Italian stallion with his shirt unbuttoned too far. He had his hands all over her. I moved Stephanie to the side so I could get a better look, but she mistook my touch for attention and dropped down in front of me, grinding into my lap. I was about to go rip that creep's hands off Zoey, but then I noticed the look on her face. She wasn't hating it.

The song turned to a slow one, and I side stepped out of Stephanie's talons before she could pull me in. I walked over to Zoey and Rico Suave. "Zoey, come on, I think we should go." I placed my hand on her elbow.

"What you're the only one who can get any action on this trip? A bit hypocritical, don't ya think?" She nodded towards Stephanie, who stood watching us, pouting.

"Zoey, you don't even know this guy—he likes look he's twenty-five."

"Fabien, Matt. Matt, Fabien," she introduced us.

He gave me a wink and pulled Zoey in close. I could definitely take him.

"Don't be a cock-block." She waved me away.

I felt Stephanie tugging at my arm. "Are you coming back?" I looked at Zoey one last time. She seemed so carefree, moving in tune with the music, smiling coyly at her Italian dance partner.

"Ah, yeah." I let Stephanie grab my arm and pull me towards her.

*****

I checked my watch and realized we had fifteen minutes to get before our curfew. I gathered everyone up and we headed outside into the cool night air. It was sprinkling outside when we started the walk back.

"Who was mister tall, dark and handsome?" Amanda asked Zoey.

"Fabien."

"Even his name's sexy," Stephanie said.

I walked ahead, a little embarrassed that I'd tried to interfere with Zoey's pick up.

"Hey, Parker —wait up," she jogged up to me.

"Hey."

We walked together in silence for a few minutes. The sky opened up and the rained poured down on us in fat, wet drops. I looked up and let the water splash down on my face. It felt good, refreshing.

"Wow," Zoey held her hands out in front of her, palms up, catching the rain.

"Come on," I grabbed her hand. I wasn't sure why, but I'd been wanting to touch her all night. I started jogging down the middle of the street, pulling her along. Our feet splashed clumsily in puddles as we ran. Zoey squeezed my hand tighter and we ran as fast as we could through the rain. The others were soon far behind us. I pulled Zoey around a corner, into an alley and held her with her back against the wall. I grabbed her waist, pulling her under the awning, away from the streams of water pouring from the blackened sky. Her eyes met mine and realizing I was clutching her waist, I pulled my hands away, quickly. I took a step back from her. We stood facing each other and our chests rose and fell heavily while we caught our breath. Water ran down her face and plastered her hair to her cheeks. Her tank top was glued to her body and she had goose bumps on her arms. She still looked beautiful and as always, her blue eyes captivated me.

"Hey, what are you guys doing? Mr. Rhinehart's going to flip if we're late," Bobby called from the street. Zoey and I broke apart and jogged out of the alley after them.

When we reached the hotel, we left squishy, wet footprints through the lobby. Instead of heading for the elevator, Zoey turned towards the stairs. "I'm gonna take the stairs," she said.

The others continued to the elevator, while I followed Zoey to the stairs. She pulled opened the fire door and started up the stairs. For the first two flights, I simply followed behind her, but when we reached the door to the third floor, I stepped in front of her before she could open it.

"Did you have fun tonight?"

"Yeah, did you?" she asked.

"Going to night clubs is definitely not a normal activity for me, but it was alright," I tried to sound cool.

"Why didn't you go with them?" she asked. "Stephanie likes you, you could probably hook up with her if you wanted to."

I shook my head. "I'm done with girls like that."

-- Zoey's smug smile told me she wasn't quite convinced. "Well, this is me." She motioned to the door. I moved away from the door so she could pass through. "Night," she said behind her.

"Night." I watched her ass as she walked away. Yeah, I would definitely be thinking about that later.

Chapter Thirteen

Zoey

Okay so maybe it was Paris' effects on me or the glasses of wine I drank last night, but Matt Parker was getting under my skin. He walked alongside me, casting his big shadow next to my smaller one. We were supposed to use our free time each day to do research for our paper, but since we still hadn't decided, instead we used the time to explore, eat, walk the city and eat some more.

Our group visited another museum, and then Matt and I had time to wander on our own. We stopped and sat in a beautiful garden, I wished I had my sketch pad. I wouldn't have minded staying there all day, but our hunger won out.

We wandered down the street for a few blocks until we found a little café tucked into a narrow side street and sat at one of the outdoor tables. Today Matt ordered for me without me having to ask then poured water from the carafe into my glass. I didn't trust the way he was looking at me. It was a foreign concept to have someone doing things for me. I felt useless. I was used to being in control and looking after everyone, but each day away from my family I got a little more used to it.

"So what schools are you applying to for next year?" I asked.

"I'm not," he said.

I studied his face, trying to interpret the comment. Maybe he'd already been offered a full ride somewhere and didn't need to apply. "How's that? You get good grades, right? And obviously you're the star of our rinky-dink town's football team."

"Yeah, my grades are fine."

"So why aren't you going to college?"

"I'm going to take over my parent's auto parts store in a few years, so I'm going to start working there fulltime next summer. I'll probably take a few business classes at the community college."

"Well, I plan to get the hell out of South Lake I soon as I can. I'm gonna apply to State and Central since they're both a few hours away."

"That's cool," he said.

"So is that what you really want to do? Stay in South Lake your entire life?" The concept baffled me. I knew doing good in school was my ticket out of here. I didn't plan to end up a forty-year-old divorcée waiting tables at the local IHOP. I wanted something better, and could never fall for a guy who wanted to stay in our small-ass hick town just for the fun of it. I couldn't wait to get out.

"It doesn't really matter, my parents need me and it's the family business. What am I supposed to do? Just walk out on them? The store was always supposed to go to me and my brother."

I didn't dare say anything that had to do with plans him and his brother had made, I knew I'd never talk of him of this. "So, theoretically, if you were going to go away to college, what would you want to major in?"

He thought for a minute. "Creative writing."

Hm. This boy confused me, sometimes he seemed like so much more than a small town jock, but then other times, like when he said he planned to stay in South Lake, I didn't know what to think.

Our pizza came and we dug in, happy for the distraction.

"So, you really think you'll be happy staying in South Lake?" I asked.

He nodded. "That's why I wanted to come on this trip, to get to see some the world while I still have the chance."

He talked like he was chained to our town. Only, I was pretty sure it was self-imposed. We finished our food and decided to walk back to the hotel rather than continue to wander aimlessly around the city.

We passed by a little girl that reminded me of Cora, and I stopped momentarily to watch her push a miniature baby stroller in jagged lines, then stop to check on her baby doll every few paces. Her brown hair flipped crazily around her face, just like Cora's did in the morning before I wetted it down and slicked it back into a braid.

"She looks like your sister, right?" Matt said, noticing.

I nodded and felt a lump rise in my throat. I couldn't worry about the kids right now. I had no control over the situation. Besides, I would be home in a few days, so I might as well enjoy my time here. We sat down on the bench across from where the girl played and both Matt and I watched her until she was too far from view.

"I liked it when you wore your hair down last night," his voice sounded soft, bringing me back to the moment. We were sitting close on the park bench and he was looking over at me. He moved his hands carefully up to my hair and I turned to face him. I felt him work my hair free from the black elastic ponytail holder I wore every day. My hair fell down around my shoulders. He put my rubber band around his wrist. It was stretched out from overuse, but it seemed to fit perfectly around his wrist. I combed my fingers through my hair, trying to understand what had just happened.

It felt like something had changed between Matt and I, but I didn't understand what. We walked back to the hotel in silence. And when we got back, we went to Matt's room, since I was pretty sure Amanda would be camped out in mine working on her homework. I sat down at the desk and Matt sat on his bed. Even though I'd been in here when I'd helped him through his migraine, it felt a little strange to be in the small room with him. I felt clumsier than usual, more unsure of myself than I was used to. That hair comment he made completely baffled me. Last night, Stephanie was throwing herself at him and he barely noticed, but he seemed to pay attention to the smallest things about me. I needed to test this theory to see if I was completely losing it.

I stretched my arms over my head, exposing a strip of bare skin at the waistband of my jeans. I had no game when it came to seduction. I wanted to do something that made his man parts bigger. I lingered there with my arms above my head like a clumsy fool. His expression was more *are you okay* than *you have my full attention*. *Great. Just what I needed.* I dropped my arms down to my sides.

Chapter Fourteen

Matt

Zoey was acting kind of strange. She sat down at the desk in my room, and flipped through my travel guide while chewing on the end of a pen. The way her open mouth worked around the pen put me in a trance. Damn, why was she so orally fixated and was it causing my sex drive to kick into action? I reached over and took the pen from her mouth.

"Can you stop that? It's a little distracting."

"Hmm?" She looked up at me and pierced me with her blue eyes.

I grabbed a book off the side table and covered my lap.

"What the fuck is that?" Zoey asked, pointing at my lap.

Shit. I was busted. I pressed the book closer to my stomach, hoping I was concealing my crotch, but refusing to look down.

She reached for the book and removed it from my lap. But

instead of focusing on the budge in my jeans, she studied the cover of the book. I exhaled the breath I'd been holding in. The blood flow started to recirculate throughout my body and I realized she was still waiting for an answer on the book.

"Is this yours?"

I nodded.

"You read poetry?"

I nodded again. She stood and walked across the room to the tiny window, still holding the book. She set it on the window sill and moved the curtains aside to look out the window.

"I write it too." I'd never told anyone that before.

"Cool." She turned and smiled at me in that way she did, raising just one corner of her mouth, so I couldn't tell if it was a smile. "Will you show it to me?"

"Um, probably not. I don't really show it to anyone." I shifted under her gaze. She took a step towards the door, almost testing her weight. I wasn't convinced she actually wanted to leave. And that thought pushed me forward. "I had fun with you today." I reached up and gave her an awkward high five. It was really just an excuse to touch her, to see if she'd let me, but the second our hands touched and then fell apart, I realized how weak my attempt was.

"Me too." She looked at me strangely. Then yawned and stretched her arms over her head again, which gave me a nice peek at her stomach , which looked smooth and flat. "Well, I guess I should get going." She started past me on her way to the door, and I'm not sure what made me do, but I reached out and grabbed her wrist.

"Don't go."

She stood in front of where I sat on the bed and waited for me to unhand her, only I didn't. My heart raced. Had the mixture of flirting and bickering all week led to this? Or had I read the situation between us entirely wrong? I knew she could probably tell I wanted to kiss her by the way I was watching her mouth, but she wasn't pulling away from me. I stood up in front of her, the height difference between us even more exaggerated at this close distance. I looked down into her eyes.

"You want me to stay?" she whispered. She swallowed and bit her bottom lip while she waited for me to answer.

I nodded. We stood like that for a few seconds more, only it seemed like forever. I knew I was taking too long. I don't know why, but she intimidated me. Should I just bend down and kiss her? Was that what she wanted me to do? Or would she laugh and push me away? I wasn't sure if I'd read this situation completely wrong, which was entirely possible.

Tired of waiting, Zoey pulled me in by my belt buckle and planted her lips firmly on mine. Once our lips met, I was momentarily stunned that I was actually kissing her, but I caught on pretty quickly and covered her mouth with mine. She was a good kisser, just like I'd imagined while watching her play with that pen in her mouth. She was more frantic than I expected, and it sent a wave of heat through me.

I pulled back from her. "Wait. What were we doing?"

"You want to talk? Now?" She rolled her eyes. "Of course you do."

I took a deep breath then pulled her to the edge of the bed to sit with me. I brushed my fingers along her cheek, involuntarily touching her again. "I mean if we mess around —we'll still have to work together and it might be weird. We shouldn't right? We're just friends."

"I didn't know you'd want to dissect it play by play. Besides, we're not friends. More like frenemies," she said.

"Frenemies?"

"Or frenemies with benefits," she added. I gave her a confused look. She pushed my shoulders back onto the bed so that I was lying down. "That okay with you?" She bent down and kissed me again without waiting for an answer. Her lips were hot and tasted like cinnamon gum. I forgot my previous argument and I rolled over on top of her and kissed her back, more deeply this time.

*****

The hour long make out session with Zoey was not nearly enough, but we had to go meet the group downstairs for a bus trip to a nearby winery to learn about the wine making process. When she left my room to go downstairs, she didn't even look back. And then, on our tour of the winery, she walked ahead of me with Amanda and Stephanie, even though I knew she didn't really like them. Zoey was quiet at dinner and didn't sit near me on the bus ride back. I wondered if she regretted what happened earlier or if it was just a one-time thing. It was late when we got back and instead of trying to go out in the little time we had left before curfew, I went to my room alone.

A few minutes later, I heard a knock at the door and found Zoey standing there.

"Can I come in?" she peeked around me to see if Bobby was inside.

I stepped aside. "Of course."

She came in and sat down on my bed. Man this was messing with my head, sometimes she seemed interested in me and other times she completely ignored me. I wasn't sure what was going on with us, but somehow, that only made me want to find out more.

"So, what's up?" I stood in front of her.

"I thought you could use a little company." She put her hands on my hips, and just that small touch sent bolts through my stomach, bringing all my senses to full attention. "Plus, I thought earlier was fun."

I swallowed.

She scooted further onto my bed and lay down on the pillow. Apparently we weren't going to talk, but I wasn't going to wait for a formal invitation. I lay down on top of her, covering her body with mine. I held myself up on my forearms, keeping most of my weight off her. "Am I too heavy?"

"No," she breathed against my mouth. I could tell she'd brushed her teeth. Damn. Why hadn't I thought to do the same? Probably because I didn't know she'd come over after ignoring me the rest of the day.

She ran her hands along my biceps and pressed her lips to mine. I kissed her back and opened her mouth. Her tongue was soft and firm at the same time and the way it lingered around mine was getting me hot. I pressed my hips into her and she wrapped one leg around my back, drawing me even closer. God, she was sexy. She wiggled her way out from underneath me, and pushed me down onto my back, straddling me. She pressed her hips into me and bent down to kiss me. She was wearing her hair down again and it fell around us, creating a curtain. She lifted my T-shirt and ran her hands over my stomach.

"Damn." She lifted my shirt to inspect me further.

"What?" I asked trying to sit up to see what was wrong.

"You have a six-pack."

"Oh." I fell back onto the pillow. "You like?" I teased.

"Very much." She smiled.

I cupped her jaw in my hands. "Come here." I guided her mouth back to mine.

The door opened and light streamed into the room. We sprang apart from each other, sitting up on the bed and straightening our clothes. Bobby stood in the doorway, looking smug.

He flipped on a lamp. "Next time, leave a sock on the doorknob man, I had no idea you had a....lady in here."

I didn't like the way he hesitated around the word *lady*, but it wasn't something I was going to address right now.

"It's cool—I was just leaving anyways," Zoey said. She hurried out of the room without looking back or saying goodbye, leaving me watching the door long after it closed.

"What was up with that?" Bobby asked, still staring at me.

I wish he'd turn away—I had a raging hard-on that I needed to adjust. I shrugged. "I don't know," I admitted.

Chapter Fifteen

Zoey

The days quickly turned into Matt and I looking for ways to be alone together. Meeting in my room after Amanda left for the day, or his room at night when Bobby was out, ducking around the sides of buildings on our walks in the city, or heading down deserted hallways of the museums we visited to get away from the group, but it never seemed like we had enough time. We were always interrupted before either of us could get our fill.

It was really unexpected the way I seemed to crave him, his very lickable lips, the way he trembled when I touched him and how he seemed fascinated by playing with my hair. He was definitely a fun plaything. My very own euro-fling. Morgan was going to shit when I told her I hooked up with Matt on this trip. It was just like she predicted. Maybe she knew something I didn't —that preppy guys like Matt liked to go slumming from time to time.

I used our hotel's ancient desktop computer to log in to my email and send a note to Ty midway through our trip. I was almost afraid to check in and get bad news about how things were going at home, but in the end, my curiosity won out. I typed a quick note asking about what was happening at home and hit send. I didn't expect to get a note back so quickly, given the time difference, but Ty's reply popped up when I was halfway through clearing out all the spam in my inbox.

Sis, things are weird w/out you. Mom's annoying me and keeps forgetting stuff, like that we need lunches packed. I'm trying to help out but you're better at this than me. When are you coming home?

Ps. Don't worry about Pete, he's doing fine.

Ty

I knew it was a strange reaction, but tears welled up in my eyes. It felt good to be needed and missed. And I was relieved to hear Pete's asthma was under control. I'd never forgive my mother if something happened while I wasn't there. When I was home in my daily rhythm, sometimes I felt invisible, like no one really paid attention to all that I did to keep the house running. My dad was clueless, since he was always at work, and the kids just excepted that I would always be there. But now that I was away, maybe they'd appreciate everything I did more now that they'd experienced what life was like without me.

Amanda found me in the little business center, hunched over the computer. "Come on, Zoey, we gotta go."

I followed her outside where the group was waiting and shared a knowing look with Matt. We both knew we'd be hooking up tonight, and it made me all the more excited to get to on with the adventure.

Our trip was more than half over and still Matt and I hadn't decided on a topic for our paper, but maybe we'd come up with something genius on the next stop of our tour.

I hung out with Amanda during the three hour walking tour of the city's architecture and listened to her drone on about how cute she thought Bobby was. Gag me. He was a pre-pubescent dwarf with shifty eyes. But they were both about a four, so who was I to judge?

*****

We arrived back at the hotel, I grabbed my room key and headed to the lobby hoping Matt had the same idea and would meet me there. A few minutes later, Matt came out of the elevator and without missing a beat, walked up and took my hand. "Shall we?" he asked, sweeping me towards the doors.

Suppressing a grin, I worked my hand free from his. He avoided meeting my eyes, suddenly embarrassed that he'd violated our arrangement. With him at my side, being in a new city didn't intimidate me. I felt like we could do anything we wanted. And we did.

Whereas the few first days had been warm and sunny, it had now turned chilly and damp, I huddled into my thin thread-bare cardigan and ignored Matt's repeated attempts to give me his jacket.

We spent hours walking the Champs Élysées, which is this huge avenue in Paris, lined with shops, cafés, and cinemas. We reached the Arc de Triomphe, and took the stairs all the way up to the top and looked out over all of Paris.

Matt was being really quiet, but that was fine with me. We stood the top for a while, just looking out at the clear sky and the city spread before us.

We were too intimidated to ride the metro back, though I knew it would have been an easier way to get around. So we turned and walked back the way we'd come from. There was so much to see along the tree-lined sidewalk, so we hardly noticed that we'd racked up so many miles.

After walking for a while, we stopped at a café and ordered cappuccinos and sat at an outdoor table. When Matt reached for his mug, I noticed he was still wearing my black elastic hair tie around his wrist, and even though I had more in my room, I was still wearing my hair down. I tried not to think about what either of those things meant. Now that we were no longer walking, the cool air gave me goose bumps through my long sleeved T-shirt.

I wasn't used to spending this much time with someone my own age and having to make conversation. At home, I rarely had to time for form a coherent thought, it was mostly just shouting commands at my siblings to do this or stop doing that, and with Morgan, I mostly listened to her stories about her latest crush.

Luckily, Matt and I felt comfortable enough around each other that neither of us felt the need to make constant chatter. But still, we hadn't said much in the last hour and it was bugging me that I couldn't think of a single thing to talk about, especially now that we were sitting across from each other and he was just staring at me.

"Using only one word, what was your first impression of me?" I asked him.

"Huh?"

I knew he'd heard me, so I just waited for him to comprehend what I meant.

"You sure you want to play this game?" He looked over at me.

"Yeah, just hit me with it." I cracked my knuckles.

"Okay." He shrugged. "I guess the first thing that came to mind was *cold.*

Cold? I wrapped my hands around the little mug, trying to draw some warmth from it.

"I don't think that anymore," he added. "But the way you distance yourself from everyone at school, I guess that was the impression I had."

"Fair enough," I said.

"What about me?" he asked. "What was your first

impression of me?"

"Spoiled," I blurted out without hesitating.

"Spoiled?" He seemed genuinely surprised.

"Yeah. You work for your dad, you drive a nice SUV, you can do pretty much whatever you want at school, or get one of your minions to do it for you." I wasn't going to mention the All-American hero vibe he gave off, his perfect clothes and skin. Or the clean, male way he smelled.

"Hmm." He considered it. "My Dad pays me minimum wage and I have to work way more than I'd like, and that truck was my brother's. I had to beg my parents to let me keep it and I make the payments now." He rubbed a hand across his hair. "And at school, I guess that's just me keeping up appearances, doing what everyone would expect."

So I had him all wrong once again. I took a sip of my cappuccino. Maybe it was safer not to talk, that way he wouldn't keep revealing things that made me seem like a bitch and him less and less like the guy I'd initially thought.

*****

At dinner that night I trailed my finger across the length of the menu until I found what I was looking for –*les entrees*. I read over each one carefully. I didn't want to repeat my horrible experience of ordering our first night in French. I studied the menu, concentrating on the individual words that made up the item. *Endives au bleu et aux noix*—I knew what that was. It was definitely a salad. I couldn't go wrong with salad, could I?

My endive salad came with bleu cheese crumbled on top. Cheese in France was an entirely new experience. It was stinky and rank, but still somehow still delicious. The salad coupled with generous hunks of baguette made the perfect meal. The food here was quickly becoming my favorite thing about Paris. Well, that and hooking up with Matt. That boy's body was seriously bangin' and I desperately wanted to make it my own personal jungle gym.

I stole a glance at him across the table, and watched him stuff a crusty piece of baguette into his mouth. I purposefully distanced myself from him in public. I didn't want anyone to suspect anything was going on between us with all the time we were spending together, and well, Bobby blatantly catching us making out. I figured it was best not to arise any more suspicions.

Matt glanced at me and gestured to my mouth, then touched his own lips. He started to lean across the table. I held my hand up, stopping him. "Parker, please – we're in public."

He pressed his lips together, suppressing a laugh. "I wasn't going to kiss you, Zoey," he whispered, leaning in towards me. His amusement on his face slowly fell when he realized what I meant. "I was just trying to tell you that you have a piece of spinach in your teeth."

My hands flew to my mouth. "Oh."

I excused myself from the table, clumsily dropping my napkin from my lap when I stood. Matt and I both bent down to retrieve the fallen napkin and bumped heads. His eyes flicked up to mine and he smiled. I attempted a half smile without opening my mouth, lest I flash my spinach-filled teeth at him again, and then scampered away towards the bathroom.

I was now used to the act of dining lasting a few hours, which only left us with a bit of time hang out when we got back to the hotel. Bobby, Amanda and Stephanie plus a few other kids were going to sit by the bank of the Seine River and drink. Matt and I joined them, but I walked behind the group with a quiet girl named Shanea I'd never actually spoken to. Why change that now? We were bundled up in sweatshirts, scarves and jackets and a carried along a few bottles of cheap red wine.

The Seine River was more of a canal, carved out through the city. We sat on a stone ledge in front of the water and watched the twinkling lights that lit up a bridge ahead, and far in the distance, the Eiffel Tower rose up above everything else around it. I felt free here, like I could be or do anything I wanted. It was a very powerful feeling.

Matt walked down to the end where I was sitting and handed me a bottle of wine.

I took a long swig while he sat down next to me. Without saying anything, I scooted over close to him, until our legs were touching, trying to get warm. He put his arm around me and pulled me close. We passed the bottles of wine around until all three were gone, and divided among the seven of us, we all had a happy buzz. On the walk back to the hotel, we made zigzagging trails through the streets and they sang our school fight song at the tops of their lungs. I didn't know the words.

We were out of breath and rosy-cheeked when we made it back to the hotel. I wanted some time alone with Matt and I know he did too by the way he lingered in the lobby, but there was nothing we could unless we were willing to be obvious about it, and ask either Bobby or Amanda to give us some privacy. We both chickened out and went our separate ways. I laid in my bed unfulfilled, un-tired and a little tipsy thinking of Matt and his soft kisses. I thought about everything I'd learned about him so far this trip, and the pieces fit together in a much different way than I expected them to.

Chapter Sixteen

Matt

We got to the Musée du Louvre just before it opened, and luckily there were only a few other people in line. Zoey and I were an efficient team, once we got inside, I got the tickets while she got a map and scoped out the layout of the place. We met back up a few minutes later. "Where are we headed?" There were several staircases leading off in different directions from the marble lobby we stood in.

She pointed to the exhibition room on the second floor directly above us. "The Monna Lisa is up there. We can work our way to it though." Zoey pulled me along, in the opposite direction of the crowds of people who were heading up to see the Monna Lisa.

Zoey lead me into a long room filled with marble sculptures of naked dudes. She walked along a head of me. She seemed most interested in the sculptures that had their junk hanging out. She'd stop in front of one, and take her time studying it, before moving on to linger over another one. I was about to head to the next room in the exhibit when I noticed she motioned to a statue of four huge men carved from limestone. They were nude, of course. She stood there in awe, her head tilted back, jaw open. I walked up beside her. "Enjoying the view?"

She glanced over at me. "I'm just trying to understand what I'm looking at here," she said with a certain playfulness in her eyes.

"Artistically speaking, of course."

"Um, no. I mean, their junk looks kinda weird, right?"

I laughed out loud before quickly recovering, remembering our quiet surroundings. "If you're that interested, I could give you an anatomy lesson later," I offered, my voice cool, despondent. I expected her to shoot me an offended look, but when she turned her head, a slow smile was spreading across her lips.

"I'll keep that in mind." She left me standing alone in front of the Satyres en Atlante, wondering what the hell just happened.

We spent several hours walking around the Lourve, though we could have spent many more.

The Louvre lived up to its reputation, it was big. Too big. After three hours my back hurt from standing at all the exhibits, so after we saw the obligatory Mona Lisa (which was tiny) and Venus de Milo, before Zoey and I snuck out of the group tour down an empty hallway, running for our freedom before Mr. Rhinehart noticed us missing.

Zoey and I sat in the park, I was writing in my notebook

and she was sketching. She didn't even try to move the book away when I glanced over. It was the little girl we'd seen in the park. The one that looked like her sister.

I was pretty much counting down the minutes until she got bored or tired or cold and we could go back to the hotel. I knew that I should be using every free minute to enjoy the city of Paris, but I would rather be kissing Zoey.

"So, what's on the agenda later?" I asked, setting my notebook aside. I couldn't concentrate on writing anyways. "More dirty Scrabble?"

She laughed. "Only if we get to act out the dirty words."

I almost choked on the air. "Um, yes. Can we go now?" I begged.

She laughed again. This was definitely not like Zoey. She closed her sketchpad and stood up. "Fine. Come on."

I was on my feet before she could finish the thought.

Chapter Seventeen

Zoey

We got on the subway and the midday rush meant it was completely full. There was only one open seat in the car we got on. After opening doors for me all day, pulling out my chair, and ordering for me, the least I could do was give Matt the seat. "I'd rather stand," I said, motioning for him to take it. I knew he was about to protest, so put my hands on his chest and pushed him down into the seat.

"Thanks," he mumbled. He lowered himself the rest of the way into the fold-down seat in the aisle. I stepped up close to him, placing my arms on either side of his shoulders to hold onto the bar behind his head to steady myself.

The crowded train car was alive with energy, filled with improbably cool and good looking Parisians. The dimming light each time the train plunged underground, the jarring and rattling that made me sway back and forth against Matt's knees that stuck out in the aisle where I stood kept me pricked at attention, soaking it all in.

The train turned a sharp corner and I stumbled to the side,

momentarily losing my balance and Matt reached around behind me and curled his fingers around the back of my thigh to steady me. I stepped in closer so that I was standing in between his legs. I knew we were entirely too close, arms and legs intertwining, but he kept his hand comfortably resting against the back of my knee, holding me in place.

The heat of the bodies all around us warmed me, and color rising in my cheeks wasn't helped by the young couple sitting next to Matt were openly making out. It wasn't like a quick peck, the kind of PDA you'd see back home, they were full on kissing. I think I caught a glimpse of his tongue. I had to look away. Something in me was curious about how people here more freely expressed their emotions, not trying to be all correct and well behaved. Like they knew how to live more fully than we did.

I stepped even closer to Matt so his knee was in between my thighs. The effect was sexy, while at the same time completely innocent. So why couldn't I get my mind out of the gutter?

He swallowed at our sudden closeness, then looked up at me. "Are you sure you don't want the seat? I feel like a dick."

There was no way I was moving. "I'm fine here."

The couple beside him only came up for air once, I noticed from the corner of my eye. And only then it was to say something that sounded impossibly sexy in French. This subway ride would be the death of me. My entire body was humming by the time untangled myself from Matt twenty minutes later.

And of course on the walk back to the hotel, I didn't get much relief from the blood rising in my cheeks. People kissed in parks, lounging on blankets together, and greeted friends on the street with a kiss on each cheek. It was like Paris was trying to break my will.

Chapter Eighteen

Matt

"Your room or mine?" she asked when we reached the hotel. She was always so down to business.

"I don't care." As long as there was a bed, anywhere was fine with me.

"Mine, then." She pulled me by my collar into the elevator. As soon as the doors closed we were kissing. She pressed the length of her body to mine and pushed me back against the wall. I tangled my hands in her hair. She smelled good, like the hotel soap and something else, kind of light and flowery.

The doors to the elevator slid open and Zoey and I pulled apart. Her cheeks were flushed and her lips were pink. She took my hand and pulled me down the hall. We jogged to her room, our fingers barely brushing. She slid the card into the door and pushed it open with her back while she tugged me by my belt loops.

It felt kind of wrong being alone in her hotel room when we were supposed to be researching a paper, but my hands moved on their own and all of a sudden, I'd pulled her close and, my hands slid down her lower back, cupping her ass and pulling her into me. We kissed for a few minutes standing like this, awkwardly in the middle of the room.

Zoey stepped back and pressed her palms against my chest, pushing me down onto her bed, then lifted my shirt and pulled it off over my head. We were actually closer to the same height with me sitting. I interlaced my fingers with hers and pulled her forward to kiss me. She worked her hands free from mine and climbed on top of my lap, wrapping her arms around my back. God, she felt good against me. I lifted her shirt up, unsure if she'd stop me, but her hands fumbled at the hem and she helped me pull it off over her head. Her bra was black and lacy, and her skin was soft and flushed pink. We shared an intense look for a second when her shirt came off. Then she was back to kissing me, her lips damp and salty on mine. We kissed like that for a few minutes, with her on my lap, and I ran my hands through her hair. I could definitely get used to spending time with Zoey.

We moved so we were lying down on our sides, facing each other, our legs twisted together. There was no part of me I didn't want touching her. I ran my fingers over her breasts and down her stomach and felt her breathing fast under my touch. I hoped she couldn't tell the way my fingers trembled when I touched her. Things were heating up fast and we pressed our bodies together frantically, grinding and grasping and moving together. My heart was beating so fast I felt like it was going to pound of my chest.

Zoey began unbuttoning my jeans and worked her hand inside my boxers. Her hands were so soft, and when she touched me, I felt like I was going to explode.

Chapter Nineteen

Zoey

I slipped my hand into his boxers and inhaled suddenly at what I discovered. He started to say something, a weak protest against my lips. "Shh. Don't talk. Don't even think." I kissed his words away and pushed him back against the bed. I didn't want him to say anything to ruin the moment. Why couldn't we just have this fun adventure together and forget all our inhibitions, forget all about who we were at home.

When I worked my hand down farther, his need to talk seemed to die away. He kissed me frantically and brought his hands to me, cupping my breasts. My breath caught in my chest. Using just his fingertips, he slowly, carefully, explored, the contour of my bra, leaving me wishing and waiting for him to push the material aside. I grew light headed in my want for him and let myself get lost in the moment.

Something wasn't feeling quite right. Not with him, this felt freakin' amazing. No, something was off with me. Things were getting a little squishy down below, and not in the good way. I pulled myself away from him and excused myself and went to the bathroom.

Not good. Dear ol' Aunt Flo had arrived, very much ahead of schedule. It must have been the flights or time change that had messed with my cycle. *Merde.*

I walked bowlegged out of the bathroom and headed for Amanda's bag, I figured she wouldn't mind my borrowing something, considering how eager she'd been to share clothes or make up.

Matt sat up on the bed. "What are you doing?"

I didn't answer, but instead flipped open the top of Amanda's suitcase and started digging through her clothes.

"Come back. I need you," he groaned and fell back heavily onto the bed. "Zoey…"

"Please hold." I held up one finger. Satisfied there was nothing in her suitcase, I moved onto her cosmetics bag, and worked my fingers around all the compacts and eye pencils, but sadly it was also free of any feminine products.

"What's wrong?"

"Slight problem."

He looked at me like he was worried. "Zoey, what is it?"

I might as well get it over with. It was just like ripping off a Band Aid, although this might be easier if he had sisters. Of course he knew how the female body worked – he'd been through sex-ed.

Just blurt it out, Zoey. He was staring at me like I was mental.

"I started my period."

"Oh." He ran his hand across his hair, like he always did. "Are you...okay?"

Was I okay? He was cute. "Yeah. I just don't have anything here."

He studied me for a second until he registered what that meant. "Oh." He was saying *oh* a lot. "Do you need me to go get you some....supplies?"

I took a deep breath, squared my shoulders, and swallowed down my humiliation. "If you could....that would be extremely helpful."

"Yeah, no problem." He was on his feet faster than I would have thought possible, throwing his shirt on over this head and checking his pockets, mumbling to himself. I thought I caught the word *pharmacie*. It wasn't like I was contagious or something. He gave me a quick peck on the cheek and was out the door. When the door clicked behind him, locking me in, I felt completely alone.

I changed into sweatpants, then stuffed a bunch of tissues in my underwear and paced the room, waiting for Matt to get back with the goods. It took him forty-five minutes. I let him in the room, more annoyed than grateful that it took him so long, but that quickly faded when I saw how nervous/ excited/ helpful he was trying to be.

"I wasn't sure what to get." He dumped a brown paper bag onto the bed. He brought back three boxes of tampons, one for light flow, one for heavy and one that was scented. Along with a green package called *serviettes hygènique*, which seemed to be pads.

"Is this enough?"

"Uh, yeah. For six months."

He smiled, clearly pleased with himself.

I grabbed a box of tampons and headed to the bathroom. When I came back, he was lying across my bed watching TV. I figured he'd be gone by the time I came out, scared off by the female crisis at hand.

"All better?" He patted the bed beside him.

I walked tentatively towards him, then sat on the edge of the bed. It took me a minute to figure out why he was still here, but then it struck me—he wanted his reward. I inched closer to him.

"Lay down," he said.

I lay next to him and started kissing his neck.

"Mmm. That feels nice." He squeezed me closer.

He smelled like Abercrombie cologne, clean and woodsy. I worked my way up to his jaw, then finally to his mouth. Our kissing started out soft at first, but once my tongue met his, I started to get into it again. I slipped my hand into his jeans.

"Wait, Zoey." He grabbed my wrist, effectively stopping my hand.

"What's wrong?"

"Nothing, it's awesome." He kissed my forehead. "It's just we probably shouldn't, you know?"

"No, it's cool—I have some tissues nearby."

"That's not what I was referring to."

I pulled my hand from his jeans. "What is it, then? I'm not good enough for you? After you've been with Chelsey?"

"What? Of course not. That first night here, you told me this was a business arrangement." He looked down and re-buttoned his jeans. "Do you even like me?"

"I like your body." I slid my hand under his shirt, caressing his stomach. "What's the problem? I thought we agreed to this friends-with-benefits thing?" I was very aware that I'd said friends rather than frienemies this time, but didn't correct myself.

"I guess," he said. "But, besides, you're on your…"

Typical male, couldn't even say the word period. "What, do I gross you out?" I pulled back from him.

"No," he said more enthusiastically than necessary. "I just feel bad I can't return the favor." He grabbed my hand and squeezed it. "I want to make sure the lady I'm with is having a good time."

That cocky grin I'd grown used to was back.

"I *was* having a good time until you interrupted us for this commercial break." I swatted him with a pillow. He grabbed it and flung it back at me. And before I knew what was happening, we were hitting each other with pillows and wrestling on my bed. It was like a kinky game of twister, and I was pretty flexible in these sweatpants. He tickled my waist and pulled me on top of him. His eyes were bright and happy and he was grinning at me like a fool. Damn, he was cute. I was going to miss this, and that scared the shit out of me.

Chapter Twenty

Matt

Zoey had almost given me a heart attack yesterday. When she'd gotten up suddenly during our make out session, my first thought was that she was searching the room for condoms. But it was a totally different product she'd been looking for. One, that for some reason, I agreed to search the city looking for.

I liked that Zoey didn't pressure me to be who everyone else thought I should be—but at the same time she challenged me in unexpected ways—to be who I wanted to be, someone who was not fake but felt like an actual human again. It was okay to be real around her, to talk about John, even to get a migraine and she didn't freak out. If she could see the darkest side of me—a side I showed no one and still like me—what did that mean?

It was our last full day in Paris, and like an omen it was pouring. Mr. Rhinehart was running around trying to pass out a revised copy of the itinerary—one he'd created for "inclement weather" but everyone was laughing and crumpling them up.

The rain wasn't keeping anyone inside on our last chance to

see the city. A group of us walked down to the Eiffel Tower, fighting our way through the crowds, and trying to avoid the obvious scammers looking for money from the rich American tourists. Whenever the wind picked up, the unmistakable smell of urine wafted by. The rain finally stopped, and the sun came streaming through the clouds, drying the dampness all around us.

While our classmates went to McDonalds and Starbucks, Zoey and I headed to the open air market and picked out French pastries—a croissant and a pear-vanilla muffin, then grabbed baguette and a wedge of soft cheese and made our way to the park.

We sat on a park bench to listen to an outdoor string-quartet concert. I set the food down and spun Zoey around and tried to dance with her. She made a throat-slashing motion at me, and I released her. I settled for sitting next to her, listening to the music while we ate.

Zoey looked longingly at the street cart selling hot pressed sandwiches. They did smell amazing. "Matt, go order me a something," she said, eyeing the food.

"You have to conquer ordering for yourself, Zoey. Just try it. I don't know what I'm doing either."

"No, you're better at it. I'll get it wrong and probably come back with an old shoe. Plus, at home I'll have to take care of myself plus the kids, so, never mind...forget it."

"What? Say it."

"It's nice having you do stuff for me."

I chuckled and shook my head, but then stood up and squinted over at the street vendor. "What do you want?"

"Something good and Frenchy." She tried to hand me some euros.

"No, I've got it," I said.

I carried back two hot ham and cheese paninis for us. We unwrapped the soggy paper and I watched as Zoey bit into hers, crunching through crispy bread, gooey cheese oozing from the sides of it. She actually moaned when I bit into it.

Chapter Twenty-one

Zoey

It had been an interesting week, and unexpected in a lot of ways. Matt continued to surprise me. And if life had taught me anything, I didn't like surprises. I needed to know what to expect, what I could count on. Growing up like I did, I craved things I could easily categorize, control and move past. Matt had turned out to be none of those things. Yet, I had liked this week with him much more than I expected to. But I knew this was all a fluke—it was the allure and mystery of Paris and each of us being out of our element that allowed us to connect. Back in South Lake, this would have never happened. We'd had fun, but now we would both go back to our lives, which certainly didn't intersect.

So it only seemed fitting that I was spending my last night in Paris doing what it was I did best—taking care of someone else. Stephanie and Bobby had dropped Amanda off sloppy and drunk and left me to balance her over the toilet and hold her hair back. *Fan-flippin-tastic.*

Done barfing for the moment, I leaned Amanda back against the bathroom wall. "Stay," I commanded, heading to answer a knock at the door.

Her head slumped to the side and rested on her shoulder. "Mmm hmm," she mumbled.

I pushed my hair out of my face, and pulled open the door. It was Matt. He was holding two chocolate croissants. "Baked goods and dirty Scrabble?"

I couldn't help but smirk. "You can come in, but I should warn you that Amanda's passed out in there." I nodded toward the bathroom.

"Is she sick?"

"Yeah, Bobby and Stephanie dropped her off drunk for me to deal with." He waited in the door way. "I probably won't be much fun tonight."

"That's okay, I was just sitting around and thought I would come find you. I could use the company."

I stepped aside from the doorway. "Enter at your own risk."

He brushed in past me and I could smell his Abercrombie cologne. My mouth started to water and I wasn't sure if it was the promise of baked goods or him.

He handed me the croissants, then turned on the TV and flopped down on my bed. It was unmade from my earlier nap and somehow it seemed too intimate to have having lying on my sheets. I stood there awkwardly, holding the pastries. "Make yourself at home."

He rolled over on his side to look at me. I set the pastries on the dresser, then went to check on Amanda. Rather than the sitting position I'd left her in, she was curled around the toilet bowl, lying on the bathroom floor. "You okay?" I poked her with my foot. She nodded without opening her eyes. "Alright, well, I'm just going to leave you here for a bit to make sure you're done. Then, we'll try some water and put you into bed."

She nodded again. "ThanksZoey." It came out in all one word.

I went back out and sat on Amanda's bed across from Matt. Not only was he taking up my entire bed, but there was that little detail that I didn't cuddle. I thought he was deep into the Italian news, watching the busty female news anchor, but he surprised me. "Sucks this week is over," he said without glancing up from the TV.

"Yeah. Listen, Matt—with her sick in there, we probably can't do anything tonight."

He glanced over at me. "It's cool. I didn't come here to be entertained." He wasn't getting the hint. I guess it was really time to make things a little more clear. We would be back in Ohio tomorrow and I felt the need to set some boundaries. Matt had gotten comfortable pretty quickly (exhibit A was how he was curled up in my bed right now) and this wasn't going to fly at home.

"Come over here." He patted the bed next to him. It was a compliment that he thought I'd fit in the six inches of space in between him and the edge of the bed, but it was not happening.

"I'm good over here." I leaned back against the headboard and stretched my legs out.

He rolled his eyes and got up. He sat down next to me and brought his hand to my jaw and looked into my eyes briefly before leaning in to kiss me. I turned my head and his lips landed on my cheek. "Matt." I put my hand against his chest, pushing him back a bit so I could breathe air free from his cologne. He studied me while the TV flashed in the background.

"Relax, will you? Why are you so tense?" He squeezed my shoulders. "Tell me what's up."

"We're not going to talk about our feelings, are we?" I wiggled away. "The thing is, this week was fun, but you didn't honestly think…"

"No, of course not," he interrupted. He scooted away from me. "I mean, can you imagine? Us together in the halls at South Lake?"

I laughed, maybe a little too hard. "Never gonna happen."

Matt smiled, but it didn't reach his blue eyes. He rubbed his hand across his hair.

"Help me with Amanda before you go?"

He nodded and followed me to the bathroom.

I tried to maneuver Amanda to standing, but she was floppy and uncoordinated. Matt stepped around me and picked her up. He carried her to her bed while her head bounced like it was disconnected from her neck. He laid her on the bed, then leaned back against the dresser and watched me straighten her bare legs that stuck out from her mini skirt. "Is she going to sleep in that?"

"I'll help her change after you go." I didn't mean it like that, but I knew it sounded like I was waiting for him to leave.

"All right then, I guess I'm off."

"Guess so," I said.

"Bye, Zoey."

"Bye." I shut the door behind him. After he left, I grabbed the hair tie from my wrist and put my hair up for the first time in days. I helped Amanda into her pajamas and then got myself ready for bed. The croissants sat uneaten on top of the dresser.

*****

The flights home were depressing, but also exciting in some ways. I couldn't wait to see the kids, to ruffle Charlie's hair, and breathe in Pete's little boy smell and to play Barbie's with Cora. My seats weren't next to Matt on our flight back, so I'd given him a fist bump and told him it was fun before boarding the plane. He'd stared blankly after me.

We landed to a sunny, cool fall afternoon, jetlagged and homesick. I powered on my cell and called my dad while we waited at the baggage carrousel.

"You're back?"

"Yeah, Dad. Can you come get me?"

"Wish I could. We've missed you 'round here. I've gotta get to work though. Takes forty minutes to get to the airport. I don't have time before work."

"Oh, yeah—okay. I'll just....figure something else out." I glanced around me at the happy reunions my classmates were having with their parents. I flipped the phone closed and lugged my big, black suitcase off the merry-go-round.

I rolled it towards the doors, and sat on a bench outside. I tried Morgan next, but it went straight to voicemail. I closed the phone and looked at the time, and realized that school wasn't even out yet. I guess I would just have to wait.

"Hey," I heard Matt say behind me. I turned and he was standing there, his suitcase at his hip. "You need a ride or something?"

While I'd hoped for a clean break and not to confuse things once we were home, I didn't have many choices. I nodded.

"Come on." He motioned for me to follow him.

"Didn't your parents drop you off?" I asked, remembering the morning we left for our trip.

"Yeah, but they couldn't pick me up today, so they dropped my truck off."

"Oh." *How thoughtful of them.*

We wandered around the lot for a while before we found his navy blue SUV. He put both of our suitcases in the back, then we climbed inside. It was meticulously neat inside and smelled like his cologne inside. It reminded me of being close to him and made me a little dizzy.

We drove in silence and when we got closer to town, I directed him to my house. I was embarrassed when he pulled up to my shabby light blue house with its peeling paint, muddy gravel driveway and crooked mailbox out front. "This is it."

He parked in the street and got out, pulling my suitcase from the back. "I can help you get it inside."

Like that was happening. "I'm good," I said, pulling my bag from his hands. "Thanks for the ride."

He nodded and tucked his hands down low in his pockets. I heard footsteps pounding the pavement —and turned to see the kids running towards us. They must have just gotten out of school.

"Zoey's back!"

I dropped down my knees and pulled them in.

Matt watched me get assaulted by Pete and Cora on the sidewalk, while Ty and Charlie eyed him suspiciously. He got back in his truck. I glanced back at him and saw that he was laughing as he pulled away.

*****

By Sunday night, I was desperately missing Paris, or at least ready to get back to school. I'd forgotten how exhausting it was being at home. Nothing had really changed –my mom barely acknowledged I was back, and when Dad wasn't working he was laid out on the couch, remote in one hand, a can of beer in the other. My little bit of solitude came when I spent Saturday afternoon at the Laundromat and then roaming the aisles of the grocery store.

Morgan had joined me for a little bit while I did the laundry and though I wanted to tell her about Matt, for some reason I held that back. .

It was ten o'clock on Sunday before I got the house back in order. There were endless piles of pajamas and abandoned socks, a mountain of Legos under the dining room table to clean up, and a dead fish floating in Pete's fish tank that needed a fishy funeral before being flushed down the toilet. I headed to my room, exhausted and unappreciated and sat down at my computer to check my email. There was nothing but junk. I logged into Facebook and saw I had a new friend request. I clicked on it. It was from Matt. I leaned in to look at the tiny picture of him, standing so proud with the football tucked under his arm. He'd typed a message.

I need to see you, he'd written. He'd left his phone number too. He'd sent it an hour ago. I closed the computer without accepting his friend request, but grabbed my phone and sent him a text. And even though it was after ten, I'd written: *K. Come get me.* After I sent it, I had a mini panic attack. He probably meant that he needed to talk to me at school tomorrow or something – about our assignment.

But my panic was short-lived, because a few minutes later he texted me back, saying he was on his way. And then a whole new wave of feeling flooded me. I rushed to the bathroom and brushed my teeth. Everyone was tucked into bed, so I made my way quietly down the stairs and waited by the front door until I saw his headlights, sprinted across the lawn to meet him.

I hopped in. "Drive," I commanded. He obeyed and pulled away, his headlights illuminating the pot-hole riddled street I lived on.

"Where to?" he asked when he reached the end of the road.

"Make a right—we'll go down to the beach."

He sped up on the main road, heading in the direction I'd

told him. He felt like my get-a-way driver from a crime scene.

My rush from sneaking out began to subside and I noticed things for the first time. There was a Coldplay song playing softly in the background and Matt was looking scrumptious as ever, in a faded long-sleeved T-shirt and jeans. Part of me wanted to ask what was wrong, why he so badly needed to see me tonight, but I thought it might be crossing some type of invisible line. I didn't want to get too personal with him. I knew that would have consequences.

He parked down at the public boat launch on South Lake, at the edge of town. I looked to the backseat, and noticed he'd folded the seats down and laid a neatly folded blanket on the floor with a single tea light candle on top. Mystery solved. He needed to get some. But wait, was he was trying to make this romantic? I blinked away the thought, and climbed into the backseat. I desperately needed to keep my perspective that Matt was not my boyfriend.

He crawled back after me and we sat facing each other on the floor. He was shy at first, like it was weird to be doing this back on our home soil. And it was. Especially since he was trying to make it into something it wasn't. We were completely alone in the dark and there was no one to interrupt us. He grabbed my hand and laced his fingers between mine. I noticed he still had my black elastic hair tie around his wrist.

"Are you done with your…" he started.

"Period?"

He nodded.

"Wouldn't you like to know."

"Tell me."

"Why are you so interested in my lady business?"

He freed my hair from the pony tail, then nuzzled into my neck, but didn't answer.

"This is it, you know. We can't keep meeting up. After this —we're done."

He didn't answer, but instead became fascinated by kissing the back of my neck, lifting my hair out of the way.

"I mean, back at school tomorrow, we're back to not knowing each other, right?"

"Whatever you say, Zoey." He chuckled and pulled me down on top of him.

Chapter Twenty-two

Matt

After dropping Zoey off, I'd slept so soundly so when my alarm went off on Monday morning, it blared for ten minutes before my mom came in and yanked it from the wall. I was surprisingly well recovered from the time difference and jet lag.

I had first period with Zoey, and Mr. Rhinehart gave us the whole period to work on our assignment. Zoey looked board and distracted. She was sketching in her pad, just putting the finishing touches on the Eiffel Tower drawing. I don't know what I expected, but it was annoying me that she was acting like nothing had happened between us on the trip —or last night.

"So, I had an idea for the paper."

She stopped drawing and waited for me to continue.

"How to avoid looking like an American tourist in Paris."

She smirked and nodded once. "Sounds cool."

"Okay, so I thought we could break it up into different

sections." I opened my notebook and read them to her. "Attire, food, demeanor, language, and sight-seeing. Five sections, two pages each and we'll have ten pages."

"Sounds like a plan."

We divided up the work and used the rest of the period to start writing the paper. At least I did, I think Zoey continued drawing. When the bell rang, she left class before I could even shrug my backpack over my shoulder.

I headed to weight lifting and changed.

"There he is!" Justin called, thumping my back.

"Hey man." I thumped him back, then shoved him off me. "What'd I miss last week?"

"We got our asses kicked by Dover last week, dog—it's good you're back." I threw my shirt on over my head and swung the locker door closed. "So, how was it? You get any ass?"

I walked ahead of him into the weight room. "No, man—it was pretty cool though."

"Cool." He nodded.

*****

The week at school passed by quickly. Whenever I saw Zoey in the halls or the cafeteria, she looked the other way or did her best to disappear.

"We gotta whoop some ass tonight," Justin said, once I reached the locker room.

"I'm in." I gave him a fist bump and a smile.

We were playing Oracle Tech tonight, and Coach wanted us to take it easy this hour. We headed outside and walked around the track once and then spent the rest of the time stretching. I sat on the ground in the front of the team, leading stretches while Coach talked all about Oracle, their past performance, their tendencies, their speed.

"There's some good guys on this team," he was saying.

I bent over at the waist, reaching for my toes in a hamstring stretch and the rest of the team followed.

"There's some big guys on this team," Coach continued. "They've got a guy named Timsley, whose rumored to be college bound."

Justin told me they'd done drills in practice that week all aimed at taking this guy Timsley down. I switched the stretch, and pulled my ankle up behind my butt, stretching my quad. The guys followed.

"All right—they're all yours, Matt." Coach Dickey tipped his ball cap at me and headed into the gym like he usually did the last ten minutes of class. The guy's eyes were on me. I switched legs and pulled my other ankle up behind me. I remembered last year, when everything seemed so much easier. I remembered getting into a circle with the guys, and the *your mom* jokes would be flying, but now they just stared at me, waiting for me to do something, anything. I clapped my hands together, signaling the stretches were over and the guys circled up around me.

I mouth went dry, and my mind was blank. The team was looking at me, waiting for me to start. They squinted into the sun as the seconds ticked by. Someone cleared their throat. I felt a bead of sweat run down my temple. My heart sped up.

Justin stepped forward. "The past three years against Oracle it's been a tough game—this year we're gonna steam roll those fuckers!"

The guys erupted in cheers, before taking off, jogging towards the showers.

"Hey, thanks man," I said once it was just Justin and I.

"You alright?" he asked.

"Yeah." I shook my head. "Must still be jet-lagged I think." We walked to the showers without saying anything else.

At the game that night, Timsley was living up to everything we'd heard. He was a beast —easily six foot five and three hundred pounds. My only tactic was to charge at him and try to take his legs out from under him. The first time I'd dropped him, which felt really good. It was right in front of the student section too, and I relished in the sounds of their cheers as I jogged away.

But after that first time, he caught on to my strategy, and he'd decided he wasn't going to be dropped by me again. After that, trying to tackle him was like running into a brick wall. It actually hurt when we collided, and stole the breath from my chest. He wasn't going anywhere. When I couldn't get him down, I just held onto his jersey and tried to drag him down. I heard the whistle and let him go. I tried to walk it off, but I suddenly had a bad feeling about the rest of this game.

At half time, we were holding on, but just barely. The team looked pretty roughed up with bloody elbows and grass-stained jerseys. I looked up and spotted my parents in the crowd. My mom waved. I didn't wave back. I scanned the faces in the student section, looking for Zoey, though I'd never seen her at a game before.

The second half of the game only got worse. I had little to no effect on Timsley, and though I tried to keep my head in the game as the clocked ticked down, the worse things got and the further they pulled away from us on the scoreboard. Coach Dickey was pissed. I pretended I couldn't hear his screaming at me from the sidelines.

After the game, I didn't say anything to the team. I threw my pads off and was the first one in the showers. I stood under the cool water and took deep breaths.

Justin followed me out of the shower with a towel wrapped

around his waist. "Hey, don't worry, man—that guy was huge."

"Yeah, I guess." We were dressed by the time the rest of the guys were done showering.

"You going to Summer's tonight?" He punched me in the shoulder. "Her parents are out of town –everyone's going. Come on."

I grabbed my bag and followed him to the student parking lot and we drove in a caravan to Summer's house.

We pulled up to a two-story house on a wooded lot, and judging by how far down the block we had to park, the place was already hopping. We went in without knocking . "It smells like skank in here," Justin said, eagerly sniffing the air, rubbing his hands together.

Someone handed me a red plastic cup of beer, but once I reached the kitchen, I set it on the counter. Chelsey was there with Dave. He sat on the counter and she was standing in between his legs.

On second thought, I picked up the beer and took a swig. I looked around and recognized a lot of people from school. On the other side of the dining room, Zoey stood talking to Morgan. She wore a navy blue sweatshirt with the hood pulled up. Her eyes practically glowed against the blue of her shirt. Even though she was out in public at a party, she still managed to set herself apart and made a point to look like she didn't fit in. Part of me was jealous that she never pretended, that she was always true to herself, not worrying about pleasing anyone.

Laughter in the kitchen brought my attention back to the moment. Justin was telling a story about a freshman he was close to closing.

"Isn't she a little young—even for you?" I asked.

Their eyes turned on me.

Justin's grin turned devilish. "If there's grass on the field— play ball." The guys busted up laughing.

I took another gulp of beer and realized the guys in the kitchen were looking at me, asking about the game.

"What happened, Capt'n?" Bryce asked, knocking back his beer.

"We got whooped like a red-headed step-child tonight," Justin said, crushing an empty can in his hand.

"Looks like Paris made Parker soft," Bryce said.

"Guess you won't be a Marine like your brother," another said.

I looked to Justin, who had a sour look on his face, knowing the comment was off, but he said nothing.

I rubbed my temples, hoping that wasn't a headache a felt

coming on. I looked over to Zoey and saw her blue eyes were locked on mine, looking worried. Without saying anything, I left the kitchen. I didn't know where I was going, just that I needed out of there. I headed towards the back of the house and passed by bedrooms occupied by horny classmates. I tried the bathroom, but the door was locked. I turned and was ready to slump down in the hallway and totally loose it, but I felt a hand on my forearm pull me around the corner.

Zoey was pulling me into a darkened laundry room. She closed the door behind us, blocking out nearly all the light, except for what came in around the cracks in the door. She placed her hands on my chest and walked me backwards until I bumped into the washer.

"What are you –"

"Shh." She placed a finger over my lips. "No talking," she whispered near my ear. She put her hands under my shirt and ran her fingertips up my stomach. It sent a chill through me. She reached up on her toes and kissed me. I brought my hands to her face, and pushed her hood back and kissed her deeply.

Being in a darkened laundry room with Zoey was way better than being out in the party. I felt so comfortable with her, and yeah, I liked kissing her too. My heart was pounding, but in a good way. I felt alive, challenged, accepted. Not like I did out in the party with my so-called friends.

"Zoey," I said in between kisses. "Hang on…can we…."

She stopped kissing me and held my chin so I was forced to meet her eyes. "I. Said. No. Talking." Then she went back to kissing me.

I didn't argue. I lost myself in her attention. She didn't care how I did on the field, that I didn't have a witty come back for the guys in the kitchen, or that I didn't have the faintest idea about what I was doing. I mean, she did only seem to want me for one thing – but who was I to complain? This is one thing I could do right. Hopefully.

Zoey scooted towards me, and pressed her chest to mine. It was pitch black but I could just make out her smirk as she wrapped her legs around my waist and pulled me in closer.

It was like no time had passed since the trip. We both remembered, or at least our bodies did. I danced my tongue around hers felt her groan as she ran her hands through my hair. She wrapped her arms around my neck and pulled me even closer. I fumbled in the darkness, and gripped her ass, pulling her closer to grind my hips into her. I felt her breath catch against my neck.

There was no air circulation in the tiny room, and I was starting to sweat. I pushed her shirt up and bent down to kiss her chest, all along her bra, when all I wanted to do was take it off, but it's not like we had a lot of privacy here –someone could barge in any second. And Zoey felt so good, I didn't know how I would stop myself with her. I must have been losing my grip on reality because when her arms closed around me, I wished we could stay like this forever.

Chapter Twenty-three

Zoey

I broke apart from Matt and fixed my clothes. I ducked my head out the open door and confirmed no one was around. I glanced back inside for one last look at Matt. "See ya, buddy."

"You have to go…*now*?" he groaned.

It almost changed my mind, but I knew the longer we stayed together in this laundry room the more likely it was that one of two things would happen – one, we'd be caught by someone and I didn't want to deal with that right now, or two – that we'd end up going all the way, and for some reason the thought of that scared me. Like it would catapult our relationship to a new level that I wasn't ready to accept.

He pulled me back in by the waist for a quick peck on the lips before I disappeared down the hall to go find Morgan. She wasn't hard to find. She was straddling a bar stool at the island, challenging some guy to do a shot with her, but when she saw me, she broke into a sloppy grin. "Where the hell have you been?" She lifted my hair off my shoulder and looked at it like it was a foreign object hanging down by my face. Which it was, she rarely saw me with my hair down, but for some reason, whenever Matt was involved my hair came down. "Someone's been naughty." She smiled. "Bedroom hair." She lifted it again to show the guy next to her. "But Jordan's outside smoking, so where the hell've you been?"

"Shh. Keep your voice down." I swatted her hand away from my hair. The look on her face told me she wasn't going to give up that easily. "Fine. Come with me." It was probably time to get this over with anyway.

Morgan hopped down from the bar stool and followed me out the front door. We sat down on the steps, and hugged our knees against the chill in the night air. Morgan was looking at me, waiting for me to start.

"So, were you hooking up with a mystery man?" she prompted.

I glanced around to make sure no one was around to overhear us. "Sort of."

Morgan clapped her hands. "Oh man, I knew it. Who is it? Braydon?"

"What? No." Braydon was one of Jordan's skating buddies.

"Who then?" She nudged me with her knee.

"You'll never guess." I shook my head. Her smile grew wider. "And if I tell you—you will need to be *sworn* to secrecy."

"I can do that." She nodded, looking at me expectantly.

"So, I kind of hooked up with Matt Parker on the trip."

"What!" She screamed, turning her body towards mine.

"Shh. Keep it down, Morgan. No one can know about this."

She clamped her hand over her mouth, her eyebrows furrowed. "And it's still happening? You two…"

"Uh, yeah. In the laundry room just now."

"Holy shit, Zoey! That boy is a fine piece of man meat." Her dopey grin was back.

I cracked a smile. "I know—trust me."

We sat in the night air, letting the reality of it sink in. "Are you guys like…what? Friends…dating…what?"

"Um, no. We're nothing. It's done," I said, but even I noticed that my voice lacked conviction.

"Yeah right. You're gonna give that up?" She nodded her head towards the street.

Perfect timing. Matt was walking around the side of the house out towards his truck with his friend Justin behind him, who was trying to talk him into staying. They stopped under the street lamp and stood there arguing for a few minutes. Defeated, Justin headed back towards us, while Matt continued down the street to his truck.

"Sup?" Morgan gave a head nod to Justin as he stepped in between us up the front steps into the house.

I waited for the door to close again, blocking out the sounds of the party, leaving Morgan and I in complete silence. "I'll admit, it was fun, and he's...okay looking."

"Okay looking? That boy is redonkulously sexy. I need details." She grabbed my shoulders and shook me.

"We actually didn't do much more than just make out."

"How much more are we talking—let's focus our conversation there." Her finger punctured the air as she said *there*.

I thought back to that afternoon in Paris—I'd wanted things to go farther, but then an unwelcome visitor had arrived and ruined everything. "It was actually pretty embarrassing. We were starting to get it on, and..." I laughed nervously and shook my head.

"What?" Morgan looked at me.

"I started my period."

"*Goo.*"

"Yeah, I know."

She made a face, showing her teeth. "You didn't like, bleed

all over him or anything?"

"Oh, God, no. He was actually really cool about it and went out to get me supplies."

"Hmm," she said.

"What?"

"I don't know, Zoey. That sounds like something a boyfriend would do."

"Psh. No. Don't get any weird ideas. We were hook-up buddies, that's all." I opened my mouth to explain that he was just returning the favor from when I'd helped him out with his migraine, but then thought better of giving Morgan any more ideas about what exactly was going on between me and Matt.

I talked Morgan into leaving a little while later, and when we got back in her Civic, I pulled my phone from the cup holder. I had a new text. From Matt. *Goodnight,* he'd written.

"Who was it? Everything okay at home?" Morgan asked, pulling the car out carefully from our parallel parking spot.

I deleted it without responding. "Yeah, everything's fine. It was nobody."

She looked over at me suspiciously, but didn't press for details.

*****

Monday and Tuesday passed without Matt and I exchanging a single word in class. Maybe he thought my no talking ban in the laundry room at Summer's last weekend was still in effect, but for whatever reason, Matt was avoiding me. I sat in the back, as I usually did and Matt returned to the front row. I did my best to ignore him and act like everything was normal between us. Though we'd decided on a topic for our paper, we hadn't actually discussed it any further.

I ducked out of class Wednesday, keeping my eyes on the floor as I squeezed past the desks in the front row. I wanted to avoid this whole, 'why did you pull me into the laundry room for a make out session last Friday' conversation we were probably going to have.

I spotted Morgan in the hall and walked with her to our locker. "Did you see him again?" she asked, wagging her eyebrows at me.

"No."

Chelsey hung on Matt's arm and tried to keep up as he walked down the hall and my eyes followed them. She wore actual coordinated outfits. Today it was short skirt, black leggings, with black sequined flats and a fitted black and white striped sweater. It looked really soft and the way it strained tight over her chest was hard not to notice. I, on the other hand wore what Morgan called *groutfits*, gray outfits. I looked down at my faded jeans and old V-neck

T-shirt that was heathered and worn thin from so many washings, but it clung to me in the right places, so maybe it was okay.

*****

After school, Pete and I walked side by side down the uneven sidewalk towards town. With Ty at soccer practice, Charlie with his friends and Cora at swim lessons for the next two hours, it was just Pete and I. And in honor of his getting an A on his spelling test, the two of us were going out to eat to celebrate—somewhere with chicken strips per his request. And bonus – it meant I didn't have to cook.

Pete was still young enough that he liked hanging out with me, whereas my other brothers saw it as punishment to have me watching over them. I felt like we were being watched and turned to the street just in time to see Matt's SUV slowing down beside us.

He lowered the passenger side window. "Hey!" he called.

I gave a head nod, and tried to keep walking. Pete tugged my hand. "Who's that, Zoey?"

"If you're lost, the interstate's that way." I pointed up ahead without meeting his eyes.

He laughed. "Hold up a second." He pulled up to the curb

157

and parked, then hoped out and jogged around to meet us on the sidewalk. "You're talking to me again." It wasn't a question.

"Maybe."

"Well this calls for a celebration. What'dya say—Chick-Fil-A, my treat."

"Can't. I have Pete tonight." I set my hand on Pete's head. He turned back and forth, looking from me to Matt.

"So we'll bring him. Man, woman and child—it'll be fun."

I gave him my best *WTF, are you kidding me* look.

"Come on. I'll teach him guy stuff."

"He's eight. Calm down on all that. I don't want you turning him into a macho football meat-head."

"Whoa. I'm offended. I have a sensitive side."

"Yeah? And where's that?" I took a swing at his stomach, but he stepped out of the way before I connected. Then he lunged at me, wrapping his huge arms around my waist and swung me up, lifting my feet from the ground. It was as though away from the prying eyes at school, he couldn't help but touch me. I pushed the thought from my mind. "Set me down!"

"You have a big mouth for someone so miniature. Are you going to be nice now?"

Pete giggled behind his hand.

"Yes," I said through gritted teeth. He set me on my feet and continued walking like nothing had happened. I flipped my foot up behind me and kicked his butt, whistling as I walked along inconspicuously. Pete giggled again.

I looked back behind me. They had stopped walking. "I'm Matt," he was saying, bent down on one knee. They shook hands. "Pete," I heard my brother say. I felt something pull inside me, something I didn't recognize. "Come on, I was promised Chick-Fil-A." I continued walking towards town.

When we got to the restaurant, true to his word, Matt paid for our order. We slid into a booth with Pete and I on one side, which left Matt sitting across from me, watching me try to eat a chicken sandwich.

"What?" I asked, wiping my mouth with the back of my head.

Matt's mouth turned up in a crooked smile. "Nothing." He pulled a fry from the carton and thought about dunking it in ketchup. "So, Pete, do you like football?"

Pete nodded wildly, half a chicken strip hanging from his mouth.

Matt laughed. "We've got to get your sister to bring you to one of my games sometime."

And that was all it took. Pete was a convert to the 'Matt's a hometown hero fan club'. The adoration in his eyes for Matt was obvious. "Yeah, Zoe. Can we go?" Pete asked.

"I've got a game this Friday," Matt encouraged.

"I don't know. We'll have to see." I tried to think of a reason why we couldn't —but there wasn't an actual reason I could come up with.

We ate in silence for a few minutes. Matt held up a limp French fry, curled over and soggy with grease. "If you knew you were going to have your last meal—what would you want it to be?" he asked, studying the fry.

I wasn't sure if the question was directed at me or Pete or just rhetorical, but it was kind dark. Pete surprised me by answering. "Mine would be a peanut butter, banana and chocolate syrup sandwich that Zoey makes me." He smiled.

"What about you?" Matt nodded to me.

"Uh, I guess something really impractical—nothing you'd never have at home." I thought about it for a second, taking another bite of my sandwich. "There was this Death by Chocolate cake I had at a restaurant once—maybe that."

Matt considered it, then tossed the fry aside.

"What about you, Matt?" Pete asked. My eight-year-old brother was not known for his conversationalist skills, so this should tell you how smitten with Matt he was.

"My mom's steak and potatoes," he said without even thinking.

"Our mom doesn't cook," Pete said.

"No?" Matt asked.

"Okay Pete, finish up—we've gotta get going," I interrupted. Enough of the family-sharing time.

We gathered up the paper wrappers and used napkins and Matt took the trays to dump in the trash can on our way out. We stood awkwardly in front of the glass door to the restaurant.

"Well—thanks for dinner. You didn't have to do that."

"It was no problem," Matt said.

"Say thank you, Pete," I prompted.

Pete mumbled his thanks and Matt returned a fist bump. "No problem buddy."

I pulled Pete by the hand and started down the sidewalk.

"Wait, Zoey—I'll walk with you."

"That's okay, we're going to take the bus. We've got to pick up my sister from swimming."

Matt jogged to keep up with us. "I'll drive you. You guys

don't have to take the bus." His eyes were soft, pleading, only I couldn't understand his motives.

"It's fine. Thanks though." He'd already done enough.

He stepped in front of me, blocking our path. "It's just—we need to work on our paper."

I stood staring at him, unable to answer, to think of a reasonable way to turn him down. "Yeah, tonight's no good." I thought about how my mom hadn't even gotten out of bed when we were home earlier.

"Tomorrow then. I'll come over."

"Sorry, I promised Cora that we'd have a tea party and color."

"That sounds good to me." He smiled.

Shit. Did he just invite himself over? And why couldn't I find the words to turn him down?

"See ya, Pete." He ruffled Pete's hair and turned to walk back to his truck without waiting for me to answer.

"Seven o'clock," I called after him.

Oh, hell no. What had I done?

*****

After dinner the next night, I tore through the house, picking up stray articles of clothes, abandoned toys and various cups and bowls left behind in the oddest places. Everyone was home tonight, making the place feel like a zoo and even my mom decided she was going to be up and about. She was in the kitchen, trying to organize the junk drawers.

I still had no idea what had possessed me to tell Matt it was okay to come over. I mean, yes we needed to work on our paper, but wasn't that what coffee shops, or libraries were for? Did I really want Matt Parker to see my home life? No. So why was I taking the chance? I wondered why I was finding it difficult to give him up. Maybe it was the memories we shared of Paris, or the desire to go back to a week where the most difficult decisions we made were picking which pastry we wanted for breakfast, or it could have been his abs. But whatever it was, that boy was like my own personal crack and I was addicted, though I knew this could only be headed for disaster.

I tidied up around the house, but upstairs, my room seemed off limits, so I just straightened it quickly by throwing my dirty clothes in my closet and cleared off my desk of old papers. My college application for State sat there, completely filled out but forgotten. I knew I should be excited about college in the fall, but every time I imagined leaving here my stomached clenched. It was more than just the kids. The thought of my mom getting worse and no one left to hold things together scared me.

I stuffed the college application into the trash can under my desk and jogged down the stairs.

"Mom, can you just stop!" I grabbed a fistful of pens from her and stuffed them back into the drawer she was hunched over.

"What's the problem, now, Zoey?" she asked, looking bored.

"I—nothing." I took the envelopes, expired coupons and junk mail she'd collected from the counter and shoved it in the overflowing trashcan beside the counter. "I have a friend coming over to study."

"That's nice." She closed the drawer, and moved to another, rummaging around inside.

"Mom, what are you looking for?" I stood in front of her. It'd be quicker and easier if she just told me.

"Oh, nothing. I just haven't gone through these drawers in a while. Thought I might clean them out."

She had to pick now to try and do something productive? I bit my tongue to avoid suggesting that she get back in bed. I knew the kids liked when she was up. I ran a soggy dishcloth across the cracked countertops one last time, ensuring all the remnants of our meatloaf dinner were gone. Mom wandered away, leaving the drawer pulled open and bursting with random papers. I tapped it shut with my hip and went to double check that the living room was still in order.

I heard a car door close, and knew he was here before he even made it to the door. My stomach fluttered with nervousness and I busied my hands straightening the afghan thrown across the back of the couch.

"You're still going to color with me, right Zoey?" Cora looked up from where she sat on the floor.

"Yeah." His knock at the door captured both our attention. "My friend from school's here and he's going to color too," I explained, weaving my way through the living room to answer the door. We didn't have any type of foyer or entryway, so as soon as the front door swung open, Matt was in our living room, face to face with my crazy family and messy house. This was a bad idea.

"Hi," he said, waiting patiently on the front step with an amused grin.

"Hi." I stood in front of him, blocking the doorway.

"Can I...come in?"

"Yeah." I dropped my arm from the door frame and he stepped inside, taking in the room around us. Suddenly I was seeing the house through his eyes, the worn gray carpeting, and our olive green couch that sagged in the middle. Why hadn't I refolded that afghan so it at least looked neater? Or better yet, why hadn't I thrown it into the hall closet? The corners weren't matched up at all, and it hung sloppily, nearly touching the ground on one side. The walls and baseboards by the front door were no longer white, marked with brown smudge marks from shoes kicked off one too many times. Why hadn't I ever thought to wash those off? Or repaint?

Matt scanned the room around us, then walked over and knelt down next to Cora.

"Hi. I'm Matt." He offered her his hand.

She looked up at him curiously, then over at me. I tried a smile, but wasn't sure if I succeeded.

"I'm Cora," she said suspiciously, then placed her tiny hand in his. He gave it a shake, then dropped it and sat down beside her. He looked completely out of place here, too big, too clean cut, smelling like cologne. What was he doing here?

"You wanna color?" she asked.

"That's the idea," he said, looking up at me.

Cora handed him a box of crayons. "You can have blue or brown. Those are boy colors."

"Sounds good to me." He graciously accepted a dark blue crayon and leaned down on his elbow to help Cora color in the princess picture she was working on.

"Come on, Zoey," Cora said, reminding me I was just standing there, starring at them. I was completely out of practice with having someone over. I wasn't sure if I should offer him something to drink, but then thought better of it....we had milk or tap water. I shut my mouth and went and sat next to them on the floor and began flipping through a coloring book, hoping for the perfect picture to distract me.

I settled for a mermaid and a seahorse. First I colored in all the spots on the seahorse's stomach, watching Matt out of the corner of my eye. He was doing the same thing, and when our eyes met, he chuckled and looked down, continuing to help Cora color in the castle.

Matt didn't seem to notice the dust bunnies in the corner, or the slamming noises coming from above us as my brothers wrestled upstairs or even that we were hunched over on the floor. He acted like all this was the most normal thing in the world. My heart rate was just starting to return to normal, and then my mom decided to make an appearance in her pink used-to-be-fluffy-but-was-now-matted bathrobe.

"Zoey, I can't find Cora's immunization records." She acted like she didn't even notice Matt sitting there with us. He sat up straighter, like he wanted to stand up and introduce himself. I put my hand on his arm as a warning.

"Do you really need them now?"

"It's just that I had them, and I then I remember putting

them somewhere because I knew I couldn't lose them, and now I can't find them."

"I'm sure they'll turn up." I went back to coloring, hoping Matt wouldn't read too much into this.

She shuffled back into the kitchen and began pulling drawers open, slamming the cupboard doors.

"Hold on, I'll be right back." I got up and went into the kitchen. My mom was digging through the papers in the trash. I went to her and took her hands in mine. "Mom, stop. Why are you looking for this right now?"

She didn't answer.

"I bet Dad knows where they are, we'll ask him when he gets home."

"No, Zoey, no!" She turned away from me and pulled open another drawer. "I'm her mom, I'm supposed to know this stuff."

"Mom," I said, getting her attention again. I turned her shoulders towards me and held onto her. She crumpled in my arms, and I knew she was going to cry before I even saw the tears welling up in her eyes. "Come on, Mom, we'll get you to your room. We'll find everything when Dad gets home," I said, even though I knew this would be long forgotten by tomorrow. I turned her shoulders towards the door and stopped. Matt was standing in the kitchen doorway looking at us. "Come on." I guided her forward, hoping to get us all out of this awkward moment as quickly as possible.

He stepped aside and watched me lead her out to the living room. "I want to read with Cora," she said in a small voice when she spotted Cora on the living room floor and wouldn't go any further. The tears were fully flowing now and she wiped them away with the backs of her hands. Cora hopped up and took Mom by the hand and guided her upstairs.

"Come on, Momma—I'll read you a story," Cora's soft voice rang out from the stairs.

I turned to Matt, who was still standing in the doorway. "Sorry about that."

"No, no problem." He took a step closer to me. "Is your mom okay?"

"Yeah. She'll be fine. She just goes through stuff like this sometimes. It's no big deal," I heard myself saying. I could tell my cheeks were turning pink.

"Are you sure everything's all right?" He took another step closer to me. I looked down, and nodded. "So, I guess we're done coloring?"

"Yeah, if that's cool with you." I sat down on the couch and put my head in my hands. Today had exhausted me, cooking dinner, cleaning, and it was all for nothing, Matt had still seen what a freak show I was.

He came and sat down next to me. "So maybe we could work on our paper then?" he asked, scooting closer to me.

"Yeah, my stuff's in my room —I'll grab it," I said, standing up suddenly.

"Can I see it?" he asked.

I turned back around to face him. "My room?"

He nodded.

He'd already seen everything else, so I didn't see the point in trying to hide my room from him too. "It's kinda messy."

"I don't care," he said.

"All right." I turned and headed up the stairs, with Matt trailing behind me.

We reached the top of the stairs, and I was all too aware of my brothers playing video games in Charlie and Pete's room, and Cora and my mom lying across her bed. I knew my mom wouldn't say anything about me having a boy up here, it was such a rare occurrence that no one knew how to act. I led him into my room and closed the door behind us, shutting us in my dimly light room.

He stopped just inside the doorway and looked around.

Chapter Twenty-four

Matt

Zoey's room wasn't at all what I expected. Nothing about Zoey was like I expected. She put off this tough-persona, but seeing her with her little sister, and her mom tonight, I was starting to realize she was anything but. She was the one who took care of everyone. I looked around her room, taking it all in. She had a twin bed with purple covers that was left unmade, the room was cramped with the small dresser and desk, but the main feature of the room were the pictures of elephants large and small, covering most of the open wall space.

"What's with the elephants?" I asked, walking around the perimeter of the room to get a better look at the pictures.

"I used to be really into elephants. My mom and I used to hunt for pictures of them in magazines, books, anywhere we could." She ran a finger across a black and white circus photo with a lady seated on an elephant's back. "I should probably just take them down," she said, dropping her hand.

"I don't know, I like them. Did Cora do this one?" I

pointed to a roughly sketched out elephant in pink marker. It's trunk was bigger than its body.

"Yeah. When she was three." Zoey went to the desk and took out her Global Studies book. "So should we do this?" She pulled out the desk chair for me, but I sat on the bed instead. I sunk down into her pale purple sheets and noticed they had tiny yellow stars on them. Zoey seemed flustered, but sat down on the chair.

We spent the next hour alternating between focusing on the sections of our paper and stealing sideways glances at each other. I kept wondering what she was thinking. It was strange being alone in a bedroom with Zoey and not grinding up against each other, but also kind of interesting at the same time.

Her mom stuck her head in to say goodnight, and seemed to actually notice me for the first time, smiling and telling us not to work too hard. She said nothing about us being alone with the door closed, or staying up too late on a school night, like my mom would have done. She just smiled and shut the door behind her.

Zoey closed her book and stretched her arms above her head. I wondered if she was signaling me that she was tired and wanted me to leave.

"So I guess once our paper's turned in on Friday, you'll be done with me," I asked, looking over at her.

She didn't answer, but instead concentrated on shoving her books back into her bag. "I'll type up my half of the paper tomorrow night and send it to you."

"That'll work."

"Would you mind printing it off too? We're out of ink cartridges," she said.

I nodded, then laid back on her bed, resting my head on her pillow.

"What do you think you're doing?" she asked.

"Getting comfortable." I smiled up at her, knowing this was bugging her. She got up and thrust my backpack at my chest. "Ouch, what was that for?"

"It's getting late," she said, standing over me.

I took her wrist, and tugged her down to the bed, knowing she'd act like she wasn't happy about it, but wouldn't argue. She collapsed down beside me, and after hesitating for a second, laid down and let me wrap my body around hers. And even though she was facing away from me, I could still tell she was trying not to smile. I turned her head gently towards mine and kissed her jaw. She laid perfectly still, letting me work my way down her neck, then she scooted closer and turned towards me so I could reach her mouth. We kissed slowly, gently for a few minutes.

I pulled back to look at her, and she opened her eyes slowly, sleepily. "Why'd you stop?" she whispered against my lips.

I pushed her hair back from her face. She looked beautiful right then, completely relaxed and happy. "You didn't answer my question from before." I hesitated. "What happens when our paper's turned in? Is all this done?"

She rolled over and looked straight up at the ceiling. She was quiet for so long, I didn't think she was going to answer. "What if we made some type of arrangement?" I waited again for her to continue. "Say we each get one more free pass. You can call me once more and I can call you once too. Then that's it. No more secret hookups. I mean, we're probably tempting fate already. I'm surprised no one's found out." She climbed onto me and straddled me. "What do you think?"

Her thighs pressed me to the bed and I loved the way she trapped me under her. "Ah. Yeah, that works." I kissed her. I hoped that after a couple more meet ups like this and she wouldn't be able to stay away from me. But somehow I knew whatever Zoey set her mind to, she would achieve.

We heard her brothers laughing from down the hall, and sat up on the bed, suddenly remembering we didn't have complete privacy.

"You're lucky you have so many siblings. With John gone, my parents only have me to focus on. I mean, didn't you notice I was the only one in class that had both parents come to that trip meeting?"

"Yeah, I don't have that problem. I hardly see my dad, with

him working nights and well my mom, yeah, not so much."

I could tell she didn't want to talk about her mom, but that only made me more curious. I dropped it for the time being. "So will you come to my game this Friday, and bring your brothers?"

She cocked one eyebrow up. "And why on earth would I do that?"

"You've never been to a game before, have you?"

"Nope," she admitted, proudly.

"Don't you think you should at least go to one high school football game before you graduate?"

She stared at me blankly.

"Once in a lifetime opportunity to see yours truly kick some ass on the field," I said.

"Didn't you lose your last game?" she asked.

"So you have been paying attention. Maybe if I had a better cheering section that wouldn't have happened." Actually, up against Timsley, I'm sure it wouldn't have made a difference. I was just glad I'd walked away in one piece. But I just wanted to see if I could actually get Zoey to go.

"I'm sure cheering fans are not what you're missing—I've seen the way girls and guys, for that matter look at you with complete worship."

"I told you, I don't really care about all that."

She pulled back and scrutinized me, checking for signs of dishonesty.

"You've probably never been to a high school dance, either?" I guessed, thinking about the semi-formal we had coming up.

She shifted and sat up, scooting away from me on the bed. "That'd be a safe assumption." She swung her legs over the side of the bed. "Come on, I'm tired." She handed me my backpack. I got up and followed her into the hall. She headed towards the stairs, but I ducked around the corner.

I looked inside the boys' room, and saw them huddled side by side on the bottom bunk, looking at a video game. "Goodnight—nice meeting you."

Their heads popped up. Pete's voice rang out above the others, "See you at the game!"

Zoey did not look amused, but I dutifully turned and followed her down the stairs while trying to suppress a smile. We stood together in the open front doorway for a few long seconds without saying anything. She looked me over, then picked up my wrist, and plucked the black elastic hair tie of hers I was still wearing. It snapped softly against my wrist. No matter what either of us said, it was clear this thing between us wasn't over.

I walked into school Friday morning with Justin and saw Chelsey standing up ahead of us waiting in front of my locker.

"Rumor has it Dave's already done with her. He got what he wanted," Justin said, under his breath, nodding towards Chelsey.

Chelsey was wasting no time in crawling back. She was leaning against my locker in her cheerleading uniform.

"Hi, Matty!" she said when we got closer.

Justin glanced at the sour look on my face, then over to Chelsey's toothy smile. "Your own your own." He gave me a fist bump and sauntered off down the hall.

"You excited for the game tonight?" she asked.

I opened my locker and grabbed my Global Studies book. "Sure."

"Me too. I'm wearing my lucky pink polka-dot boy shorts." She smiled. "You remember those, right?"

"I've gotta get to class, Chels." I shrugged my backpack strap over my shoulder and turned to leave.

"Wait, Matt." Chelsey grabbed my hand, stopping me. "I was just wondering…are you planning to go the semi-formal?" She smiled up at me, still holding my hand.

"Chelsey." I hung my head, trying to think of a way to get rid of her.

"Yes, Matt?" she asked, hopeful.

"You cheated on me, remember?"

"But that was a mistake." She gave my hand a squeeze.

Zoey chose that moment to walk by, looking from my face down to Chelsey's hand in mine. I quickly dropped it. I wondered if I'd just seen disappointment in Zoey's eyes before she ducked her head, letting her hair fall into her face and walked off towards class.

I headed into class and set our paper down on the corner of Mr. Rhinehart's desk.

Zoey didn't even look my direction, even when I leaned over to let her know our paper came out really good. She nodded just once while looking straight ahead at Mr. Rhinehart. Then reached back and secured her hair up in a tight bun.

At first break in the commons, Chelsey scooted in next to me on the bench seat and walked her fingers up my thigh. I slid over out of her reach, so our legs were no longer touching, and bit into my granola bar, doing my best to ignore her.

Zoey was across the courtyard, standing under the oak tree with her friends. I was too far away to hear what they were talking about, but everyone was laughing—except Zoey. I had to sit there watching Jordan put his grubby hands all over her. He snaked his arm around her waist and clutched his fingers into her lower back to guide her in toward him. I hated seeing him touch her. Hated it. He bent down to her ear and whispered something that made her swat his arm. Zoey stepped out of his reach. At least she never did that with me. I grinned and Justin was looking at me strangely.

"What are you zoning out on?" he asked.

"Nothing," I lied.

*****

At lunch I stood in line, waiting for pay for my grilled cheese and fries and spotted Justin sliding in to our usual corner booth. I handed the lunch lady a five and after she made my change, she winked and placed an apple on the corner of my tray.

"Here—growing boy like you. Take this."

"Uh, thanks." I turned for our table and ran smack into Chelsey.

"Matty, I'm sorry we didn't get to talk earlier."

I shifted my weight, balancing the tray with one hand. "Yeah, listen, now's not a good time." I nodded towards the table.

"The guys are waiting for me."

"Well, it's just that we didn't get to talk about the dance." She placed her hand gingerly on my forearm. "Don't you want me by your side when you're being recognized at the banquet?"

I saw Zoey walk into the cafeteria with Morgan and once again Chelsey was touching me. Zoey's mouth tugged down, her eyes narrowed as she looked at us, but she kept walking.

"Can you take your hand off me?" I asked. Chelsey pouted, but complied. "I'm not taking you to the dance. And right now, I'm going to sit with my friends." I stepped around her and headed over to Justin and a few guys from our varsity team. This definitely beat sitting with Chelsey and her judgmental friends, commenting on what people were wearing or their unfortunate bangs.

Chelsey was still standing motionless where I left her in the middle of the cafeteria. I set my tray down at the table, then walked across the room to where Zoey sat. Her friends fell silent when I approached their table.

"Hey. Can I talk to you for a second?"

Zoey stared up at me, but seemed unwilling or unable to answer. Morgan elbowed her in the side. "Mar-ci," she said through gritted teeth, still smiling up at me.

Zoey blinked at me several times. "Uh. Sure. Talk." She glanced around at her friends, indifference on her face.

"I meant just me and you. It'll just take a second." I flashed her my most dazzling smile. It had no effect.

"Whatever you have to say, just say it."

"Are you sure you want all your friends to hear what I've got to say?"

Her cheeks started to grow pink. She pushed her tray back and got up from the table. Once I was sure she was going to follow me, I walked towards the open cafeteria doors and stopped just outside them. I could tell we'd attracted somewhat of an audience on our walk through the cafeteria, and those that had noticed Zoey and me together were craning their necks to watch us through the doorway.

"What are you doing?" Zoey hissed at me.

I hadn't realized she'd be mad. "I just didn't want you to get the wrong idea—about me and Chelsey I mean."

"What? That's what this is about? This is why you make a scene dragging me through the cafeteria?"

"I thought you were mad and I just wanted to explain Chelsey and I aren't getting back together. I had fun with you the other night."

"Matt—I don't care about you and Chelsey," she said it slowly, making sure it sunk in.

"You didn't talk to me during Global Studies. You wouldn't even look at me. Something was definitely bugging you."

"Yeah, the fact that you keep insisting on trying to be friends at school. It's kinda weirding me out. It was easier when you were in your circle with the jocks and I was in my circle."

"I don't get you, Zoey. I thought we were having fun together."

She shifted her feet further apart and put her hands on her hips. "We were. Until you got all clingy. We'll keep having fun *outside* of school if you'll just not to talk me *inside* of school. Get it?"

"No," I said. "See you around. My lunch is getting cold." I turned and left her standing there. I headed through the cafeteria doors, and the hushed room came back to life with people leaning across the tables to talk, looking between Zoey and I. I slunk down low into the seat next to Justin. There were about four fries left on my tray.

"What the hell was that, bro?"

"Nothing. I just had to talk with her about an assignment," I said.

He looked me over and smirked. I knew I wasn't all that convincing, but did little to try and cover it up.

Chapter Twenty-five

Zoey

I hated myself for it, but I felt just a teensy bit mad at myself that I'd been a bitch to Matt. He was a sweet guy —which was exactly why he shouldn't be hanging around someone like me. But he seemed unable to stay away and I couldn't explain why I'd suggested we could hook up just twice more —at each of our choosing. I guess I wasn't quite willing to cut him loose, even though things were growing increasing more complicated by the day. Which was why, as I bundled the kids up in sweatshirts and jackets, I still couldn't believe I was actually going to the game.

I ran back up the stairs, leaving the kids huddled by the front door. "Zoey, come on. We're gonna miss kick off," Ty called up to me.

"One sec," I called from the top of the stairs. Inside my room, I yanked the pony tail from my hair and tore the brush through it, glancing in the mirror to make sure I had worked out all the clinks. I tossed the brush on my bed and jogged downstairs. "Ready," I declared. For what, I had no clue.

*****

The game wasn't really what I expected. First of all —I was shocked to discover that you had to pay to get in. I mean, we got the discounted student rate, which was only two bucks each, but after paying for all five of us, that pretty much cleaned me out. Now it made more sense why I'd unknowingly boycotted this high school tradition.

We made our way to the bleachers, and sat in something called the student section. I didn't know how all this worked, but luckily my brothers seemed to have a boy gene that made them instantly know what to do. I followed behind them up the bleachers, holding onto Cora's hand. We squeezed in next to a group of kids I recognized from school, but had never talked to. They looked harmless enough, I just hoped they kept their language clean around the kids.

The game started and I searched for Matt on the field, and found him. He was number thirty-six, and looked confident and athletic out on the field, moving past other guys, knocking into the other team's players, and jogging down the field. But I quickly became bored and spent the next three (yes, three!) hours alternating cheeks to try and keep my butt from falling asleep. I thought about all the things I could be getting done at home, from chores to college applications, to nice, hot bubble bath, but my brothers were having fun, and knowing this was definitely the one and only game I was bringing them to, I was glad they were enjoying it.

I tried to decipher the scoreboard, and thought we were winning, but couldn't be sure. I seemed to be the only one who was confused. The crowd jumped to their feet, or cheered or let out collective groans, other than that I could never tell if what was happening on the field was good or bad.

When the final seconds of the game ticked down, we got up and stretched, stiff from sitting on the metal bleachers and made our way out towards the field.

"Matt! Matt!" Pete called, waving his arms over his head.

Matt jogged over to the sidelines to meet us. "Hey! You guys came."

He looked cute in his uniform, bulging in all the right places. His helmet was tucked under his arm and his hair was damp with sweat at his temples. He smiled at me, and I knew all was forgotten about our awkward cafeteria run in. I bumped my shoulder against his.

"What are you doing tomorrow?" he asked.

I shook my head. "Nothing. You?"

"We should probably put our paper together since it's due on Monday."

"Is that your free pass?"

"No. This is just for our paper, I swear." He held up his hands in mock surrender, but that sexy grin on his face was damn hard to ignore.

"Mat-ty!" Justin came up behind him and tried to get Matt in a headlock, but Matt was too quick, ducking under his arm and pushing him away. "Hey a group of us our going over to Bree's tomorrow. If we help her older brother pull their dock out of the lake, he'll buy us beer."

"Sounds cool, but I'm actually trying to make plans with Zoey."

Justin suddenly seemed to notice me and four smaller versions of me starring back at him. "Okay?" he said, confused. "See ya, then." He jogged towards the locker room.

Matt turned back to me. "Should I pick you up —that way you don't have to take the bus?"

"I can just email you my section of the paper. You can copy and paste it in That way you can still do the lake-beer thing."

"Oh. All right. That'll work too." I listened for disappointment in his voice, but couldn't pick up any. "See ya." He turned and jogged after Justin, leaving me standing there, staring at his ass as he jogged away.

"Ready, Zoe?" Cora tugged my hand.

"Oh, yeah. Come on." I led the troops back home.

*****

The anticipation of using my free pass with Matt was almost better than actually doing it. I kept building things up in my mind and I knew it was stupid to think of him that way. We'd both be moved on soon. But that didn't stop me from thinking about his big, callused hands that trembled when he touched me, and the way his breath felt against my neck or the sweet way he was with my little sister.

The Matt I thought I knew from school was always ready with a cocky grin and an easy laugh –nothing seemed to get to him down. Only if what I'd seen was true, there was another side of him that he kept hidden from everyone else. A side he'd shown only to me. It made no sense, we hardly knew each other. But hadn't I done the same thing letting him come over? If Morgan knew, she'd flip.

But what I needed was help figuring this out. It was time for an intervention. I called Morgan and told her to meet me at the twenty-four hour coffee shop later that night.

Morgan was waiting at a table with two mugs of black coffee with a huge pile of sugar packets in front of her. I slid in across from her.

"Spill it." She smiled.

I emptied three sugars into my coffee, then stirred, thinking about where to start. "Matt seems to…still be interested in me. It's weird, because I thought it was just the trip —the fun, sexy ambience of Paris, ya know?"

She nodded, encouraging me.

"I don't know what's going on right now." I picked up my coffee, and brought it to my lips.

"Okay, let's break it down. When's the last time you saw him?"

I blew into my coffee and took a sip. "The other night."

"Did anything…happen?"

"We were just working on our paper, then I saw him at the game tonight. I took my brothers," I added quickly.

"Hm. I bet I know what's going on here." She tapped her finger on the table, her nail clicking. "Boys are very predictable, Zoey." She nodded, evading my unspoken question. "You guys haven't gone very far yet, right?"

I shrugged.

"A guy like Matt isn't going to walk away from a challenge unfulfilled. He's probably used to getting what he wants."

I wasn't following.

"He hasn't gotten off yet," she said, less subtly.

"Ah." I nodded in understanding.

"He wants your lady juice. It's like ingrained in males —like part of evolution, ya know?" Morgan took a loud sip of her coffee, sucking it over the rim of the mug. "They have this need to spread their seed, mate with as many females as possible. It's practically instinct. We can't really blame him, ya know?"

He stopped things that day in Paris —not me. But Morgan knew much more about sex and teenage boys than I did. She was still looking me, waiting for my response to her theory. I shrugged. "I guess so. That does make sense."

She smiled, clearly proud of herself. "So, are you going to indulge him in this fantasy?"

I looked down into my coffee while my stomach swirled uneasily. "Undecided."

Chapter Twenty-six

Matt

I was sore and tired and had homework to do, but that didn't mean my parents would let me out of working tonight. During the week, the store was open until nine, though it was usually pretty slow. I sat at the counter, hunched over my Pysch book. The bells on the door chimed, and a guy in overalls stopped and admired a display of motor oil my mom had spent the afternoon setting up in a pyramid formation. He approached the counter, looking confused.

"Can I help you?" I asked when he got closer.

"John?" He squinted at me.

"No, I'm Matt."

"Is John back from Afghanistan yet?" He picked at the top of his head.

His dull brown eyes, moved over me, taking in our similarities, waiting for me to answer. "Ah. He..." My palms started to sweat and my heart thumped unevenly in my chest. "Brandon — take over," I called to the other counterman we had in the store. He stepped in front of me while I fled to the back, just in time behind the rows and rows of dusty auto parts and hid in the bathroom. I slid down, my back against the door and drew in deep breaths, slow and steady.

I didn't come out for nearly half an hour, until I could be sure he was gone. Whoever he was he had known my brother, but not well enough to know about his death. Brandon didn't question me. He'd heard the guy ask for John and practically winced along with me. I left shortly after that, but because I knew I couldn't go home yet, or my parents would hassle me about leaving the store before closing, I drove in circles through town. Eventually, I found myself on Zoey's street without really meaning to be. I stopped and parked and held my cell phone in my hand. I wanted to call her, but didn't want to use up my one free pass.

I was still looking down at my cell, deciding what to do when I felt it vibrate. I flipped it open. There was a new text from Zoey.

Where are you? Wanna play? It said.

I waited for what felt like a semi-reasonable time, then texted back with, *Yeah. I'm here. Come down.*

I saw Zoey peek out of her bedroom window to be sure I was really here. She came out the front door a few minutes later, shaking her head with a smug, little grin on her face.

"Stalker, much?" she asked, sliding into the seat next to me.

"I was in the neighborhood." It was actually the truth. I pulled out onto the street. "You hungry? Should we grab a bite to eat?"

She scowled at me. "This is not a date. It's a hookup, Matt."

"I know that," I recovered. "So, this is your official last booty call, right?" I smiled over at her, trying to keep my composure.

"Something like that."

"Did something happen? At home, I mean?" I kept my eyes in the road, giving her space.

Zoey shook her head. "I just needed a distraction. I could've called Morgan…but then I remembered your abs…and they won out."

"Good to know." I couldn't help but smiling. Zoey was exactly the diversion I needed too. She used me to forget about the bad parts of her life and I used her to remember the good parts of mine.

Without even thinking, I drove us to the lake access and dusk settled in around us. My truck bounced along the potholes and ruts as I made my way down the dirt road along the lake. I pulled into a spot partially hidden under the locust trees and cut the engine. Then it got really quiet. I wiped my palms on my jeans to dry them. I didn't like that this was one of the last times I'd be hanging out with her.

"Shall we?" She motioned to the back seat. Just like the Zoey I had grown to know, she wasted no time in getting down to business. She crawled to the back without waiting for me to answer and I, of course, followed her. We sat cross legged in the back breathing the stuffy air, listening to the silence. As much as I wanted to kiss her, I knew as soon as I did, it would start the beginning of our end.

"So why'd you text me? Did something happen earlier?"

She looked down and picked at the hem of her fraying jeans. "Just...my mom," she said softly. "My mom happened."

I put my fingers under her chin and lifted it to meet her eyes. She looked vulnerable right then, like I'd never seen her before. I knew she would have told me if I asked, but I didn't want her to have to relive whatever it was that had happened at home, just like I wouldn't have wanted to relive what happened to me at the store an hour ago. I ran my fingers along her throat, down to the back of her neck and pulled her into me, kissing her lips softly. She didn't respond at first, but then all of a sudden, she was on top of me, knocking me back, thrusting her tongue into my mouth, pressing her body against mine. Her breath was hot on my lips, my neck, making my heart beat faster.

I held onto her waist and let her overtake everything else, all my thoughts, all my senses were consumed by Zoey. I hated her silence, her refusal to tell me what had happened, her focus on only getting one thing from me. Well, I didn't hate it that much. Blood starting rushing from my head to my crotch, making it difficult to form coherent thoughts. Especially with the way she was tracing her fingers along my thigh. My inner thigh.

I needed to take control of the situation quickly, or it would be over before it started. I rolled her onto her back and laid down on top of her. I pushed her shirt up and felt her breasts beneath my palms. Zoey moaned and worked her hand into my boxers. *Gah.* I shuddered. Her movements weren't timid at all —she knew her way around one of these.

Chapter Twenty-seven

Zoey

Matt got really quiet. He wasn't making noises like Jordan had when I'd done the same thing I was doing now. Then again, Jordan had been embarrassingly loud and made really ugly faces. Matt seemed much more in control —too much so in fact. It wasn't like I was going to demand he *say my name, bitch*, but a friendly indication I was doing this right was all I was looking for. "Are you...liking this?"

"Oh God, yes," he groaned and it sent my heart pounding harder than before if that was even possible. "I'm just...concentrating," he added.

"On?" I wondered aloud.

"You know ...on not...." He looked down at his lap.

"That's kinda the point. I want you to."

"Oh." He put his hand to the back of my neck and guided me in to kiss him. After a few minutes his shoulders trembled and he jerked forward, then smiled against my lips.

Just like Morgan predicted, things were over pretty quick after that. After he cleaned up with one of his socks and threw it out the window, we crawled back up to the front and he started the truck. He pulled it into DRIVE, but with his foot still firmly on the break, he leaned over and kissed me on the cheek. "Thanks." He smiled stupidly at me. I faced forward and stayed silent on the ride home, wondering what the hell I was doing with Matt Parker and I'd be walking into once I got back home.

I hadn't told Matt, but my mom was worse than ever. Cora had sprained her wrist that afternoon after school climbing to the highest branch on the tree in our backyard on a dare. She'd fallen and I'd spent a couple hours at the emergency room with her. When I got home, everyone was crabby and waiting for dinner, my mom the worst of them all. After dealing with all that, I just needed the distraction I knew only Matt could provide.

I tried not to think about the fact that I suggested we only see each other twice more and I'd just used up one of those. I had a feeling he would be helpful to have around all year. But I didn't want him to get the wrong idea about things. I knew things eventually needed to go back to the way they were between us before our trip to Paris. Things at home were getting out of hand and sometimes I wondered how I was ever going to get out of this town.

*****

"Brian asked me to the dance," Morgan beamed, walking beside me through the hall. "You should come —it'll be like a group thing."

At least she wasn't still holding onto delusions of Jordan and I together. "I don't think so Morgan. At this point, I want to hang onto my perfect record of never having attended a high school dance."

"You can borrow a dress from me."

"No, that's not what I mean." I looked over at her, wondering how in the world that's what she construed from my lack of interest in organized high school social events.

"It's our senior year, Zoe. We need to experience everything we can before it's all done."

Only, she didn't understand that was exactly what I was waiting for – all this to end.

*****

"What are you getting in Calculus?" Matt asked, leaning over toward me in Global Studies.

"An A."

"I could use some help studying for midterms. Could you come over Sunday?"

"Is this it then, your official turn...the last time?"

"No." He shook his head, mouth turned down. "My mom will be home. This will really just be Calc homework. The last time...we'll have to make sure there's no parental supervision."

So he was clearly interested in what Morgan had said he was. It explained why he was still hanging around. And why wouldn't he be? He was a guy. I'm sure Jordan would still be doing the same thing if I was at all interested in him.

"Uh, okay. Sure. Calc."

"Sweet." He turned my hand over and wrote his address on my palm.

I clenched my fist closed when he was done. Why did it feel strangely like he'd marked me as his?

After school, I headed off toward the elementary school, but was momentarily distracted by what I saw on the football field. Matt was leading the pack of jocks in a drill. They were decked out in their pads and helmets, but I would have recognized that cocky strut anywhere. They ran from one end of the field, tackling a big punching bag thing at the end. Matt was fast –faster than the other guys. They jogged up to him, patting him on the butt as they went by. I couldn't help but smile and slow my stride to watch for a few seconds more. He glanced up just then and caught me watching. I shielded my eyes from the sun and stared right back at him. He looked at me a few seconds too long, until another player on the team slammed into him, knocking him to the side. He jogged to join up with the others.

I had a weird feeling spread throughout my stomach. How was I supposed to tell Matt that our façade of acting like we didn't know each other at school and then hanging out at night was giving me whiplash, leaving me totally confused? I couldn't possibly admit that. I was the one who'd been calling the shots, but he'd been totally fine with it too. I had made it clear this was all I wanted—all I could handle. Only now I wasn't so sure. I had a boy who liked me, siblings that loved me and a mom who needed me. But what did *I* want? If I wasn't taking care of everyone else, I didn't know what to do – how to just be me and be okay with myself.

*****

Sunday at ten after one, I pulled onto Matt's street, where every house looked the same and the trees saplings compared with my side of town. I double checked the address I'd written down and slowed in front of his house. It was a neat and tidy spilt-level with spotless green lawn and beige siding, just like all the others. I parked my dad's car in the street, not wanting to spoil the look with his faded old Dodge. I slug my backpack over my shoulder and headed up the winding sidewalk edged with perfectly groomed shrubs. I rang the doorbell and waited.

His house was spotlessly cleaned and smelled like laundry detergent. I didn't see either of his parents, though he'd said they would be home. At first I was envious of how clean his house was, but as I looked closer—the perfect vacuum lines in the white carpet, the spotless countertops and sparkling sink, it was utterly silent with white and beige as far as the eye could see—I started to change my mind. It felt like no one lived here. I would take my messy, lived in house any day, filled with people I loved over rooms that I wasn't sure I should walk into; less I mess up the vacuum lines.

After getting us some lemonade, which he placed squarely on the coasters on the coffee table in the family room, we sat down and flipped open our Calculus books. I started with the material that would likely be on the midterm, and wrote out an equation. I pointed with the end of my pencil as I spoke. "X is the independent variable, Y is the dependent variable and B is the Y-intercept. Got it?" He looked confused, but nodded.

After more talk of tangent lines, equations, functions and limits, I could tell his interest was waning. He was staring down at the page as I talked, but the look in his eyes was faraway. "Matt?"

"Sorry. I wasn't listening."

I flipped my book closed. "I have other things I should be doing today. Never mind."

He held my shoulders, preventing me from getting up. "I'm sorry, Zoey. Stay. Please stay." His eyes pled with me silently.

I settled back onto the couch and he removed his hands from holding me in place. "Why are you so distracted?"

He stood up suddenly and pulled me up by my hand. "Come with me."

He walked down the hallway filled with pictures of him and his brother growing up, portraits taken when they were chubby and hairless, to sports pictures and school portraits, ending with a photo of John in a Marine uniform. I stopped in front of the picture. The resemblance between Matt and John was undeniable. Same square jaw, bright blue eyes, same Adam's apple. Matt circled back and stood next to me. "You guys look alike." I felt him nod beside me, and then watched as he ran his hand across his hair again.

"You want to see my room?" he asked. I didn't answer, but let him pull me away from the picture. We passed by his parent's room, its main feature a pink bedspread crisply tucked in around the bed. Matt led me into his room; it was filled with stacks of books, CDs, and folded T-shirts lined up on the floor. If I hadn't known better, I would have thought they had just moved in and he was still unpacking.

"What's with all the stuff?" I sat down on his twin size bed covered with a navy blue comforter that was soft and faded.

He sat down next to me. "Most of it was John's. My mom

turned his room into a guest room, and I didn't want her throwing anything away."

On top of his night table was a bottle of vitamins and a folded up section of the newspaper. I looked closer—the obituaries. I picked it up. "A little dark, don't you think?"

He took it from me. "I like reading the obituaries and trying to figure out what they're not telling you. Like for instance, they don't mention the cause of death if it was AIDS or suicide. Sometimes you'll understand pieces of their life—like this one." He pointed at a two inch square and read, "He finally succumbed after a long battle with cancer."

"Well, John was a war hero, so I'm sure his read well."

"He didn't have an obituary published. My mom wanted to keep everything quiet—pretend like it never happened."

I considered that for a moment. Maybe that made death easier to accept, but it seemed that all Matt wanted to do was keep the memory of his brother alive. I wanted to ask what he missed most about this brother, but his body language was rigid, unsure, like he had something bigger on his mind. I held my breath. I could practically see him trying to figure out how to put into words what he was thinking.

"So I was thinking about my last pass to see you, and I wanted to propose something different."

I waited.

"You might not like it —but just hear me out. Actually I know you will not like it." He took a deep breath. "Come with me to the dance."

I pressed my fingers over his lips. "Stop. Talking." I laughed, uneasily, shaking my head.

"I'm serious," he mumbled out around my fingers, it came out sounding more like, *mime-mirrorious.*

"Shh. No. That is the dumbest idea ever."

He took my wrist and lowered it from his mouth. "Just hear me out, Zoey."

I sat back and waited. This oughtta be good.

"As you once pointed out—I'm the captain of the football and wrestling teams. I have an image to uphold. I'm expected to go to the dance." I rolled my eyes, but he continued. "And I don't have a date. I don't want to take someone that I'll just have to try to put on an act for. If I take you, I can be myself, we'll both have fun and it'll even count as my last official free pass, so then you can be done seeing me."

I exhaled heavily, slumping with my back against the wall. Why was he so hard to say no to? "I don't have anything to wear," I said, not meeting his eyes.

"We'll take care of that. No problem. Should we go to the mall?" he asked, sitting up straighter.

"Good Lord. That's where I draw the line. Settle down. Morgan can probably loan me something."

"Cool. So, you'll come?"

"What about tickets…hair…….nails… corsages….I don't have money for any of that."

"I'll get the tickets, so that covers that. Just wear your hair down how I like it. Corsages?" He strummed his fingers on his knee. "We don't need 'em. Don't worry about that. They're kind of pointless if you ask me." He picked up my hand and looked at it. "Nails," he said out loud, as he thought. "Wait here." He got up and jogged from the room.

When he returned he was holding two bottles of nail polish. "Pink or red?"

I looked him over trying to figure out what he was intending.

"That's all I could find in my mom's bathroom."

Matt was waiting for my answer, standing there smiling at me. I was no good at painting nails, just ask Cora. I looked into his eyes. They were crystal clear blue and shined brightly at mine. "Whichever you like better," I said in a soft voice.

He looked between the two bottles like he was considering it for the first time. He vigorously shook the pink, then unscrewed the top. He looked over, studying me for a second before pulling my feet into his lap. "We'll start with your toes. They have to match, right?"

I didn't answer.

I rested my feet across his thighs. He bit his lip in concentration. His fingers looked too big holding onto the little wand, but he dipped the brush inside and carefully spread the polish across my toenails. I had a weird feeling in my chest as I watched him work. It took everything I had not to pull back from him and make up an excuse to leave the house.

He switched to my other foot and his mom made an appearance in the doorway. Even though the door was most of the way open, she made a point of pushing it open the rest of the way.

"Matt?" She scrutinized us both. "Introduce me to your friend." Her eyes travelled along my legs, which were stretched out across her son's lap.

Matt stuck the brush back in the polish and straightened his shoulders. "This is Zoey."

"Hi." I tried a smile, but it felt wrong.

"Hello." Then she turned to Matt. "Be careful you don't spill that polish." The she turned and left.

Matt resumed painting my nails once she was gone. When he was done with my toes, he painted my fingernails to match. He took his time, making sure he was staying within the lines. It reminded me of the time he'd colored with Cora. His brow crinkled in concentration, and he sat hunched over my hand. Something told me he liked the distraction, not having to think about anything else. I didn't want to tell him that the polish likely wouldn't last all the way till next weekend without chipping, but I could probably have Morgan touch it up.

"So, this dance thing...*if* I go with you. What does that mean?"

"I don't know. What do you mean?"

"We're done after that right? I mean, things are going to go back to normal, like how they were before."

"If that's what you want, then yeah."

"Hm." I considered it. "What do *you* want?"

He shrugged and used the excuse of a second coat of polish on my nails to keep looking down. I swear he had painted over the same nail at least six times.

"Basically my friend Morgan has this theory —that guys see sex like a challenge and that's why you're still seeing me. We haven't done it yet."

"Yet?" He paused from painting and met my eyes beneath

his eyelashes.

I swatted his arm. "I'm just trying to test the validity of her theory. Say a guy and a girl are messing around. Basically, is he going to stick around until he achieves the main event?"

He finished polishing and screwed on the lid while he thought. He leaned back and rested against a pillow, like this was the most natural conversation in the world. "Probably true for a lot of guys —but not all."

"Elaborate."

He brushed his hand across his hair. "Yeah, Justin, other guys I know —sure. That's the general thought process. If you're asking about me, then no."

"Why 'no'?"

He took his time, thinking about how to answer, looking deep in thought. "I had the chance to do it with Chelsey, but I didn't."

"Why not?" I felt like a broken record asking him all these questions and hoped he wouldn't read into it that I cared more than I did.

"I just knew it would mean something different to her than it did to me, and I didn't want to have to deal with that."

I interpreted both what he said and what he didn't say. He

didn't want to confuse or hurt Chelsey —since she was girlfriend material, whereas I was just some girl, so he had no such qualms about what sex would mean between us. It would be fun, plain and simple.

Chapter Twenty-eight

Matt

Morgan was attacking Zoey in the hallway. She giggled and applauded while Zoey glared at her. It could only mean one thing — Zoey had told her about the dance. I tried not to smile while Morgan threw her arms around Zoey's neck, hugging her, before Zoey pushed her away.

I knew Justin would give me shit if I told him who I was taking and I just wasn't ready to listen to it —or defend Zoey under his scrutiny. It wasn't that I had changed my mind about taking her. I just didn't feel like telling anybody about it right now.

As usual Zoey avoided me in the halls all that week. The one time she did lean over to talk to me in class, I thought she was going to say she'd changed her mind about the dance, but instead she said she'd meet me in front of the gym at nine on Friday night after my game. I still hadn't told Justin who I was taking, but today was the day. Everyone would see me with her Friday, and it's not that I was ashamed to be seen with her —I was just so used to doing what everyone expected me to. Bringing Zoey to the dance would be anything but expected.

At lunch though, I couldn't avoid telling Justin any longer, since we were both standing in line to buy tickets. I'd already heard Justin was taking Samantha Avery, a pretty junior on JV cheerleading. But just to get the conversation out of the way, I asked, "So who are you taking?" We stepped forward in line.

"Sam," he said, smiling. "You?"

Moment of truth. I cleared my throat. "Zoey."

"Who?"

"That girl I went to Paris with."

"Interesting choice." He nodded his head slowly, looking me over. "She really got under your skin, huh?" He studied me.

"Something like that. I just figured she's low key. I won't have to worry about impressing anyone."

"And she'll probably be grateful enough that you're elevating her social status to kindly return some favors."

I laughed, but nothing could be further from the truth when it came to Zoey. But I didn't explain that to Justin.

*****

The day of the dance, I shared knowing looks with Zoey all throughout Global Studies. We got our paper back —we'd gotten an A and Mr. Rhinehart had even written on the title page, *Interesting premise!*

The anticipation of tonight made me nervous and excited. It would be my last time hanging out with Zoey, which sucked. But I always had fun when I was with her. I hoped out first public outing wouldn't be awkward and we'd have fun. I wondered if we'd dance. I wondered what Zoey would wear and if she'd be up for going to Justin's party with me after. I'd brought my dress pants, shirt and tie to school in my duffle bag, since after the game, I would shower and change before meeting Zoey.

The school day passed slowly, and even during the game, I couldn't quite get myself into it. We won easily against West Branch, twenty one to three, which was nice. In the showers, I relaxed, I was finally getting ready to see Zoey. I let the hot water roll down my back. I pictured Zoey in a black dress and couldn't get my mind off the idea that she'd wear her Converse sneakers with it. But I knew she'd wear her hair down like I requested. I looked at my wrist. I still had her black elastic hair tie on.

After toweling off, I checked my duffle bag one last time to be sure I still had our tickets tucked into the side pocket and hurried to get dressed so I wouldn't keep Zoey waiting. I had to re-tie my tie three times; it kept ending up either too long or too short.

On my way out front to meet her, I passed by the gym and

looked inside. It was all decked out in streamers and balloons, like we were supposed to forget this was the place we shot hoops and ran circles when it got too cold out. The DJ was playing some crappy pop song, but no one was really dancing yet anyway. The lights were turned low and there was even a disco ball hanging from the ceiling, making everything look glittery. I stuck my hands in my pockets and strode to the door. These shiny, black dress shoes were already uncomfortable, but it would all be worth it when I saw Zoey. I knew it was weird, but being with her always made me feel better.

I stepped outside so I'd be waiting on the front steps when she walked up. I leaned against the railing with my hands in my pockets and began to wait. People started to filter in, passing by me on the stairs. I hardly recognized them, in their suits and dresses. The guys high fived me as they passed, then their hands hovered at their date's lower backs, or shoulders. Soon, that would be me with Zoey and I hoped I was man enough to take being seen with her as my date.

I kept checking the watch I rarely wore. Zoey was running late. My foot had fallen asleep and rather than continuing to stand here like a moron who was getting stood up, I went into the dance. I couldn't miss the athletic awards they gave out before the dance kicked into full gear. And for the first time I started to worry that she wasn't going to show. She'd probably changed her mind about this whole dance and last time seeing me thing.

Chapter Twenty-nine

Zoey

The night of the dance, I made an early dinner, then scrubbed out the bathtub and took a long bubble bath and generally took my time being girly, something I practically never did. I lit candles along the edge of the tub, washed my hair and shaved my legs. I was in my room putting the finishing touches on my makeup when a blood-curdling scream interrupted the process. I ran downstairs and into the kitchen where the yelling was coming from.

Charlie was hunched over the kitchen sink, holding his arm. "What happened?" I pulled his arm closer to inspect it.

"I was trying to get mom some juice, but I dropped the glass."

There was glass littering the countertop. It must have hit the counter and shattered on impact, sending the shards flying. Charlie was freaking out, trying to pull his arm away from me. By now, we'd attracted Cora's attention. She did not react well to blood and started crying.

"Ty, take Cora upstairs. Everything's fine, Cora," I said in my calmest voice.

Shit. How did you know when a cut needed stiches? I couldn't call Morgan, she'd be at the dance. My mom wouldn't know, and I didn't have time to Google it, with our impossibly slow Internet connection. I held Charlie's forearm up to inspect it. The cut was small, but deep and it had been oozing blood for the past several minutes. "Come on –we're going to the ER." *Frick.* This would mean we'd been there twice in two weeks. I hoped we didn't get turned in for child abuse. I helped Charlie put the too small Band Aids—the only size we had over the cut, trying to keep the skin together and slow the bleeding.

I didn't even bother to change out of the black dress Morgan had let me borrow, but did throw my raggedy gray hoodie over it and slipped into my Chucks without untying them. Charlie and I walked to the end of the block, and mercifully didn't have to wait long for the bus. On the way there, I repeatedly tried Matt on my cell. He didn't pick up. I knew he was done with his game by now. He must have gone into the dance. I pictured him waiting for me in his suit and hated that he thought I was standing him up. Maybe we could get through the ER quickly, or maybe they'd send us away without stitches, just a sturdier bandage.

No such luck. There was over an hour wait to Charlie to get four stitches. It was nearly eleven by the time we got home. I got Charlie a glass of milk and some cookies and helped him change into pajamas, being careful not to bump his arm. I wondered if Matt would still be there, and whether he was having fun, having moved on and forgotten about me, or if he had just left after I hadn't showed. I guess I needed to know. Plus I wanted to explain what happened and that I hadn't ditched him.

Forget wearing the strappy sandals I has planned on, I left on my tennis shoes and jogged to the school. I heard the music coming from the gym before I even pulled open the front door of the school. The hallways were dim, with just the emergency lights overhead casting everything in shadows. It always felt strange to be at school after hours. I turned towards the gym and stepped out of the way of a group of kids chasing each other out through the open gym doors. I approached the doors slowly. I hoped I could spot Matt, if he was even still here, before going in, or possibly find Morgan and have someone to walk through the gym with. I felt really out of place standing here alone in my wrinkled party dress while everyone around me danced and laughed without a care in the world. It didn't take long to spot Matt. He was standing on the far side of the gym, directly across from me, leaning with his back against the wall. I took a deep breath and started to take a step forward, but then I followed his gaze to a group of girls dancing in front of him. I looked closer and saw Chelsey seductively swaying her hips from side to side as she sashayed her way across the floor to Matt. He was leaned back, standing with one foot propped up against the wall behind him and Chelsey used his position to her full advantage. She lowered herself in front of him, grinding down the length of his body as she went.

My heart fluttered erratically. My palms started to sweat

and my fingertips went numb. It was a stupid reaction, but in that moment, my body betrayed me. Chelsey continued her dance, brushing her chest across his as she moved around his body. His face was unreadable, but he did nothing to stop her. His buddies caught onto what was happening and started hollering at him under their cupped palms.

Matt looked from Chelsey to them and then over to me. As soon as our eyes met, I felt like I'd gotten caught doing something wrong. And like a genius, I turned and ran from the gym.

I could tell Matt was behind me without even looking back. His footfalls met mine, and I could practically hear Chelsey's huff. Once I was outside, I took off in the opposite direction of home. I wasn't ready to go home. I walked through the parking lot, lit only by the florescent street lamps.

"Zoey, wait!" Matt called behind me. He quickly outpaced me and jogged around in front of me, blocking my path. I didn't stop in time, and slammed right into his chest.

Opfh.

"Will you stop?" He took me by the shoulders. I could smell his cologne, igniting my senses, making me dizzy.

"What's the point? *This* doesn't make sense." I motioned with my arms between us, causing his hands to drop away from me. "Just go back in there with Chelsey and your friends where you belong."

I turned to leave, but Matt grabbed my wrist, and held on. "No way —you don't get to say that. You stood me up tonight."

I'd forgotten that this was what he would've assumed. That didn't mean what I saw with Chelsey in there was okay —especially when I was supposed to be his date tonight. A couple ducked around us, laughing as they snuck from the dance to a car at the other end of the lot. I suddenly remembered we were in a parking lot —where anyone could see us.

I refused to believe that I had actually started to fall for him. We were too different. Besides, hadn't I always said high school relationships were stupid, and now here I was having a public fight, making a scene outside a dance? I didn't even know who I was anymore.

"What's that?" Matt pointed at my sweatshirt. I looked down and saw I had dried blood and iodine on my sleeve from holding Charlie's hand while they gave him a shot and sewed him up.

"I had to take Charlie to get stitches. I didn't stand you up."

"Oh." His voice was soft.

My heartbeat quickened in my chest. I was flooded with a wave of emotion I didn't expect. And I looked him over more closely, white button down shirt, sleeves rolled up to the elbows, tie knotted loosely at his neck, and flushed cheeks from the stuffy gym. I took a deep breath. "And then when I finally get here I see my *date* getting a lap dance from that trash whore." I shook my head. "You know what? It doesn't even matter. This whole thing is stupid, I mean what are we even doing? You're a townie, you're always going to be a townie —and I'm leaving after this year."

He stood his ground, staring at me with a look in his eyes I'd never seen, breathing through his nose while a vein stood out in his neck. "You're telling me you're really going to leave those kids? Your mom?"

I tried to say something, but the words stuck in my throat.

"I saw the college applications in your room, those were supposed to be sent in by now." He shook his head. "Quit acting like you're something your not —you're too afraid to do anything Zoey. You hide in your shell at school, you're afraid to really feel something for me. You act like a martyr, taking care of everyone but yourself. You put up a good act, but you'll never get out of this town either."

I turned and ran away from him, and this time, he let me.

Chapter Thirty

Matt

The next two weeks passed by in a blur of school, football practice, and nights spent working at the store. Zoey and I made equal efforts of ignoring each other, which actually wasn't too difficult, considering all the practice we'd had over the years. The only problem was, I didn't seem to fit in my old life anymore. I'd been stupid to think that this thing between Zoey and I would lead to something real. But without her around to sidetrack me, things sucked more than normal, plus my headaches were back with full force. Food seemed tasteless, I as distracted during football and even Justin couldn't make me laugh.

Zoey missed the next two days of school, which made it easier that I didn't have to see her, yet did nothing to remove her from my thoughts. After I football practice, I took a cold thirty-second shower and left with my clothes clinging to my still damp skin. I needed to get out of there —I couldn't take one more minute of the laughter, the practical jokes, the guys who were once my teammates and friends now just felt like intruders. It was annoying to be around people who thought they knew me so well, only they didn't.

I was supposed to go to work, but my truck wouldn't seem to head in that direction. I drove around for a while and ended up at the cemetery. I hadn't been to John's gravesite since the funeral. I was too chicken to go see it now, and just sat in my truck. I pulled some napkins from the glove box and tried writing a few things, but nothing came out right.

By the third day of Zoey being gone, I wondered if something had happened, and found Morgan at first break. She was standing with Jordan under the oak tree, the once blue streak in her hair now a freshly dyed bright pink.

They both turned and stared as I walked across the commons towards them. "Hey Morgan."

"Hi," she drew it out, suspiciously.

"I worried if you knew where Zoey was?" Morgan's eyebrows shot up and Jordan looked like someone had taken his lunch. "I just —we have an assignment due in Global Studies," I lied.

"Oh," she said, looking more relaxed. "She said her mom's been sick. But I could pass a message along if you needed me to."

I nodded. "That's okay, thanks."

I hadn't missed football practice in four years, but after school, I made an excuse with Coach Dickey that I had a migraine and needed to miss practice, then I drove to Zoey's. When I pulled up to her house, I almost chickened out. It seemed more sad than usual, dumpy and old. I hadn't noticed that before.

I walked up the rickety front steps and noticed the paint peeling from the front door. I knocked and waited a few minutes, sensing that I was being watched. It was probably Zoey, swearing under her breath that I had come. And just when I thought no one would answer, the door inched opened.

Zoey pressed her face into the open space and glared out at me. "Yes?"

"Hi." She made no move to open the door or invite me in. So this is how it was going to be.

"What are you doing here?" she asked.

"You weren't at school. And Morgan said your mom had been sick. Is everything okay?"

"Just go away, Matt." She moved to shut the door, but I wedged my shoe in the door jam.

"Wait, Zoey."

"Sorry—you can't be the hero and save the day this time." She pushed the door shut, and I pulled my foot back just in time from being crushed.

The door closed abruptly in my face, but I couldn't erase from my mind the hollow look in Zoey's eyes, the fractured sound of

221

her voice. She needed help and once again I was stuck trying to think of a way to get her to let me in. I balled my fists at my sides and walked back to my truck. I hit the gas and sped off, not sure where I would go.

When I pulled up to my house, my mom's car was in the driveway. *Shit.* I walked into the kitchen and set my bag in a chair.

"What are you doing home?" she asked.

"I was coming down with a headache, so coach let me out of practice." She stopped loading the dishwasher and just looked at me. "Mom, we need to talk."

"What's up?"

"Come sit down." I pulled her by the hand and sat her down at the kitchen table. I turned a chair around and straddled it, facing her.

She wiped her dishwater hands on her jeans, and waited for me to start. I wasn't sure if she was nervous or just drying them. "Don't tell me that you got a girl in trouble, Matthew."

"No, Mom, it's nothing like that."

Her shoulders visibly relaxed. "Okay."

I took a deep breath. "Why don't we ever talk about John anymore?" I could tell that's not what she wanted to hear and was fighting an urge to go back to loading the dishwasher. She shifted in her seat. I took her hand. "Mom?"

She didn't answer, but I read the expression on her face. It was just too hard to remember.

"I don't want to act like he wasn't in this family. I don't ever want to forget him."

She nodded. "I can try, if that's what you need."

We sat in silence for a few minutes, still holding hands. "Remember that time when I was ten and fell off my bike after trying to keep up with John and his friends and he tried to give me stiches himself rather than telling you guys?"

She nodded. "He was always a little reckless." As soon as she said it, her smile faded a bit.

"I'm just glad you walked into the bathroom before he actually sewed my forehead with pink thread. I would probably have a Frankenstein scar if you hadn't caught us."

She squeezed my hand, then let it go.

"Mom, there's something else too." I swallowed. "There's this girl."

"So there is a girl."

"Yeah. But it's complicated. I want to be with her, but she's trying to deal with some family stuff…and I don't know how to help – or if I even should."

She nodded. "It's hard for boys your age to figure out what girls need you to be. They just want to feel special – like someone cares. Like someone notices who they are, and what they need and steps up when the time's right."

I thought about what Zoey needed, even if she was too proud to ask for it herself.

"What kind of family stuff?" she asked, interrupting my thoughts.

"Her mom needs some help. Kinda like you did after John…" I stopped myself there to choose my words more carefully. I cleared my throat and started again. "Could you help me to get her into see your doctor?"

She squinted, studying me. "Are you sure you should get involved in this?"

"No. But I've got to try and help."

"Okay." She stood up and fished through her purse, handing me a business card. "This is Doctor Lowenstein's card."

She called the Doctor's office and due to a cancellation, he happened to have an appointment open that afternoon, if we could make it there in the next half hour. It felt like a sign. Now if I only I could get Zoey to listen to me. I knew it was time to tell her my secret.

*****

Ten minutes later I was knocking on Zoey's door for the second time that day. She pulled the door open this time, glaring out at me. If it was possible, she looked more frazzled than she had a half hour ago. Her hair was falling loose from the pony tail, and she kept glancing nervously back behind her, as if she was waiting for her mom to come barreling into the room any minute.

"What now?" she demanded.

"There's something I never told you."

"As much as I'd love to share a moment with you right now, Matt—I can't." The sarcasm rolled off her and she made a move once to again to close the door in my face.

I stepped in past her before she had the chance to. I looked around. It was eerily quiet in the house and I wondered if anyone was home. Compared with the bright sunlight outside, the house was dim and in need of a cleaning. I heard a low moan from down the hallway and met Zoey's eyes. For someone who was normally always in control, I could instantly tell something was wrong. Her face showed shame, failure and embarrassment.

Her mom's muffled voice called from don the hallway, "Zoey, there's not someone here is there?"

Her eyes darted past mine to the hallway. "Just a sec, Mom.

I'll be right there." Then she turned to me. "Why are you here? To see me fail? To watch the drama? I'll pop you some popcorn—you'll have a front row seat."

I stepped towards her and took hold of her shoulders, pulling her in towards me. I thought she'd fight me, but she let me fold her into a hug. "Shh," I breathed against her hair. She tucked her head under my chin. "You don't have to do everything alone, Zoey. I came to help." She stayed limp in my arms, not pulling away, but not wrapping her arms around me either. We sat down on the couch, facing each other.

"Tell me why you haven't been at school."

She looked down and picked at her nails. I knew Zoey and knew she hated admitting weakness. "My mom's really losing it—and I couldn't leave her alone."

I looked her over more closely and I wondered if she'd even showered in the last few days. "Things have gotten worse?" I asked.

"Yeah," she whispered.

"Zoey, there's something I never told."

"Matt, I'm sorry – I can't do this. I don't have time to talk about us right now."

I shook my head. "No, that's not it. I never told you about how John died." She looked up and her blue eyes pierced mine with trust. "He killed himself." I had never said those words out loud

226

before and they nearly stuck in my throat. "He couldn't live with himself after the things he'd seen and done in Afghanistan." Zoey reached for my hand and squeezed it. "And knowing that I might have been able to do something, to try and get through to him somehow, I'll never stop wondering what if..."

"It's not your fault, Matt."

I nodded. "I know that. But, we need to get your mom help, okay?"

She nodded.

"After John's...death, my mom was a wreck. She went to this doctor." I pulled the card from my pocket. "And it really helped. She got someone to talk to and some medicine that helped her deal with everything."

Zoey pulled back. "Don't think we've tried that? My mom's been on drugs before—they've never worked."

"I'm no expert, and I don't know if this'll work—I only know that it helped my mom. Maybe they didn't try the right drugs or the right dosage before—but we can tell all that to the doctor."

"We?"

"Your mom has an appointment." I glanced down at my watch. "And we need to get going if we're going to make it."

She stood suddenly, stepping back from me. I didn't know

if she was angry with me for getting involved or going to thank me for helping. But her shoulders dropped and she released a breath she'd been holding in. "Okay." She shrugged, like she'd given up on summoning the energy to argue, the effort of it too much.

"Okay." I stood up and pulled my keys from my pocket.

A few minutes later, she'd gotten her mom dressed and into her coat, and left a note for the kids, who would be home from school any minute. I drove them to the doctor's office and waited in the truck while they went inside.

Whatever happened with me and Zoey, I was glad she knew my secret and I just hoped this would work for her mom. With the ghost of John's past haunting me, I knew that was no way to live and I didn't want Zoey living with just a shadow of her mother, when it didn't have to be that way. I didn't want her to have regrets like I did over what I should have done.

Chapter Thirty-one

Zoey

My mom was getting better every day. The shine in her eyes was back, and the last few days, she'd been up to get the kids breakfast and off to school. And when we got home from school, she was up and showered, making snickerdoodle cookies or hot chocolate for a snack.

I had my mom back, though I couldn't help feeling like I had been rendered virtually useless. I used to think my family was keeping me from being a normal teen, but if what Matt said was true —it was *me* keeping myself from what I wanted. And now that I didn't have endless chores, meals to prepare or kids to take care of, I was forced to face that reality. I hadn't been who I wanted to be. I pushed people away and lied to myself about what I really wanted.

I knew what I needed to do. I picked up my phone and waited for the ringing to stop and the familiar voice I needed to hear come through on the other end. "Hey—can you come over?"

A few minutes later, I was pulling open the front door and inviting Morgan inside. She pressed her palm to my forehead. "Are you feeling okay?"

I didn't even push her hand away. "I am feeling better than I have in a long time. And this is long overdue." I took her hand and pulled her up the stairs to my room.

We sat on my bed and I came clean to my best friend about all the things I'd kept hidden. Matt telling me his secret had given me the courage to tell mine. I told Morgan about my mom, and all the pressures of taking care of my siblings, and how I never mailed my college applications in because I was afraid of being away from home, and how I'd accidentally fallen for Matt along the way. She just waited, listening quietly and pulled me into a hug when I finished. I let her hold me, making up for all the hugs I'd wiggled my way out of over the years. Maybe I was getting better at this hugging thing too.

"It's not too late, you know." Morgan pulled back and sat cross-legged on my bed.

I didn't know if she meant it wasn't too late for me to go after Matt and tell him how I really felt or that I still had time to get my college applications in, or maybe both. I didn't think things could go back to the way they were between Matt and me—he knew way too much about me and my family life. Though I had a sincere appreciation for him and always would, it would never again be fun and carefree between us and I didn't know how to handle that. I had spent so much time telling myself I didn't want something serious and that high school relationships were stupid, I had truly started to believe it. He had helped me save my mom, and it was good to have her back, so I had no regrets about our little arrangement.

I walked Morgan out a little while later and when I came back inside, my mom called me from the kitchen. "You got a letter." She motioned to the table, where the mail sat in a neat stack. I flipped through until I saw it. An envelope from the university I had never applied to. I walked, numb up to my room, holding the unopened letter in front of me. I rummaged through the waste basket under my desk, where I expected to find the college application I'd tossed aside a few weeks ago. It was no longer there. I sat down on my bed and tore open the envelope, and slid the crisp letter out.

*****

Before I even knew what I was doing, I was running. My arms and legs pumped hard, propelling me towards the school. I reached the practice field out of breath, not even noticing the chill in the air warning that winter was nearing. I hadn't bothered to put on a jacket, but right now, with the adrenaline coursing through my veins, I didn't need one. I spotted Matt on the field and watched the play the team was in the middle of. He tackled one of his teammates, then when the play was over, reached a hand out and pulled the guy up to his feet. A few of the guys spotted me standing on the sidelines and stopped to look over at me, obviously wondering what I was doing here. I saw Justin slug Matt in the shoulder to get his attention. Matt turned towards me. He pulled his helmet off. Their coach blew his whistle and let them grab a water break and Matt jogged over toward me. He stopped in front me, looking better than he had in a while, eye's sparkling and clear.

"Hey," I said, looking down at my feet.

"Hi." He looked straight at me, making the nerves in my stomach dance around.

He was quiet. I pulled the letter from my back pocket and showed it to him. "I got into State." A corner of his mouth tugged up in a smile. "Which is weird, because I never sent in my application."

"I saw it in your trash and mailed it in for you." He shrugged, then took it from my hands and looked at it more closely. "You *just* got your letter?"

I nodded, trying to decipher what he meant.

"I got mine last week," he said. My mouth opened, and I looked at him, confused. "I'll take over the store eventually, but I talked to my parents and told them I want to study creative writing."

In that moment I felt proud that he'd taken control of his destiny, and partly, he'd taken control of mine too when I needed it. I could see the guys lining back up out on the field and his coach pacing from side to side, waiting for his star player to get back out on the field. "Well, I just wanted to thank you –for everything." I took a mental image of his chiseled features, his bright blue eyes and his hair, which he seemed to be growing out, and then turned to let him go.

"Hey Zoey," he called. "I never got to use my last pass." I turned around and faced him once again. It took a second to register what he meant. "Only this time, we're going to do things my way."

"Oh yeah?" I challenged.

"Yes." He took a step towards me and closed the gap between us. He leaned down and kissed me, brushing his lips softly against mine at first, then bringing his hands to my jaw and tilting my head to meet his mouth and the kiss deepened. I felt his tongue push past mine with an urgency only our time apart could have triggered. I was only vaguely aware of the cheers of the football team as they watched us.

When we broke apart, Matt grinned his cocky smile at me. "Be ready for dinner at seven on Saturday night."

I nodded, not trusting that my voice wouldn't waver.

"Oh, and Zoey." He reached back and took the elastic band from my hair, freeing it to fall around my shoulders. "Wear your hair down."

He jogged back to the field to the cheers of his team and I didn't even try to suppress my smile as I turned to walk home.

*****

Made in the USA
San Bernardino, CA
18 April 2013